SIDETRACKED

BILL MUIR

SIDETRACKED

by Bill Muir

Sidetracked

Bill Muir

Methinx Publishing

MeThinx Publishing

Methinx Publishing
methinxentertainment.com

Printed in the United States of America
First paper edition by Methinx Publishing
ISBN: 978-1-7347696-9-2

Art & Design:
Contributing Editor: Kathryn Tedrick
Cover Art: Digital Coast Media, LLC

Chapter One

Twenty-four-year-old Katie Stevenson, a well-dressed woman with beautiful long brown hair, walked down the middle of a dark, single-lane road in a peaceful, deserted neighborhood in Kentucky. Tall, stately maple trees lined the roadside, creating a charming canopy. As she walked, Katie's light blue eyes were constantly drawn to the missing person posters attached to many of the telephone poles. The images of several pretty girls smiled, making her wonder if they, too, had been out at night, walking alone when they were snatched. She nervously increased her pace until a rustle from the bushes she had just passed startled her. Katie's breath hitched in her throat, and she stopped and spun around, staring intently into the shadows. But if someone was hiding there, she could not see him. Feeling a chill, she wrapped her arms across her chest for warmth and walked even faster. Her footsteps increasing to a rapid pace as fear shot through her veins, increasing her heart rate.

When Katie finally reached the sidewalk that led to the porch of her small, cozy Cape Cod home, someone peeked around the drapes through the front window of the house. Spotting her, the person grinned and hid, the anticipation of what he was about to do, making him feel almost giddy. Katie was relieved to be home, and she forgot her nervousness and playfully entered the dark house, closing the front door behind her and locking it.

"Mom, I'm home!" she shouted as she shook off the pall of fear and sighed with relief.

There was no reply. The steady tick, tick, tick of the living room wall clock was the only sound that broke the silence.

"Mom?"

Katie reached for the light switch near the door and flipped it on, but the room remained in darkness.

"Mom," she called out after flicking the switch several times. "The fuse must have blown again. We should really think about replacing the fuses with breaker switches."

She walked through the archway leading into the adjoining kitchen. She was about to call out again when she spotted a note lying on the counter, reflected in the moon's bright rays that streamed through the window. Katie sighed and crossed the room. Setting her purse down on the counter, she picked up the note and read it by moonlight.

Out with Ted. Don't wait up. Love, Mom

A smiley face had been drawn on the bottom of the note. Katie smiled and crumpled the paper. Then without looking, she tossed it toward the wastebasket. The wad of paper bounced off the lip of the trash can and unknowingly landed in front of a pair of muddy boots belonging to the intruder. She tried the switch to the light over the kitchen sink, but the result was the same as it had been in the living room. She remained in darkness. Katie walked across the kitchen to a cupboard and opened the door, straining to see the outline of a flashlight that had been placed on the top shelf.

As she stood on her tiptoes and reached up, the intruder quietly moved closer. Her straining fingers touched the edge of the torch, and she wondered why her mother had set it so far back on the shelf. The intruder moved closer until he was standing almost right on top of her as she finally managed to grab the flashlight. Snatching it from the shelf, she turned it on, but as she brought it down, the intruder reached out and wrapped his arms around her, pinning her arms to her sides. Katie screamed and began kicking and struggling as fear once more shot through her bloodstream. The faces from the posters outside flashed through her mind, and suddenly, she saw another poster with her picture plastered to one of the empty telephone poles. The image filled her with terror, and she continued screaming and struggling to get free.

During the tussle, Katie dropped the flashlight. It bounced off her shoe and hit the floor, spinning around several times and bathing the kitchen in a sporadic effect. Her cries were met by laughter, and she struggled even harder until the prowler released her. Spinning around, she frantically looked for something to defend herself. Still, when she looked into the face of the intruder, she realized that he was her boyfriend, Jason. He laughed again as her expression went from terror to outrage. Katie punched him in the shoulder.

"What do you think you're doing?" She screeched.

Jason reached down, grabbed the flashlight, and held it under his chin, trying to make a ghoulish face. "Ah, come on, Katie, it was just a joke."

"A joke? Have you seen the posters plastered on nearly every telephone pole in town? There's a serial killer out there murdering innocent women, and you thought it would be funny to sneak up and grab me?"

She hit him again, more to relieve the adrenaline rush coursing through her veins than for any other reason. "What are you doing here, anyway?"

"Your mom's out, isn't she? I thought that, well… you and I could…," his voice trailed off, and he wiggled eyebrows.

But Katie wanted no part in it. She opened a drawer, pulled out a short, fat candle and a lighter, and lit the wick. "She could be home any minute, and you know she doesn't think much of you." She set the candle down on the countertop.

Jason ignored her remark. "Did your mom run out of fuses?"

Grabbing the flashlight from him, Katie listened to the sound of a car coming down the street, and she grew calmer. "You'd better go. If Mom finds you here, she'll have a conniption fit."

Jason slumped off, disappointed and frustrated until Katie smiled and called after him.

"Hey."

He turned without saying a word.

"Mom's got another date tomorrow night."

A huge smile lit Jason's features, making her giggle. Katie retrieved the flashlight and set it on the counter next to the candle before following him into the living room. Still grinning, he wiggled his eyebrows once more and left through the front door. She watched him through the picture window, wondering why her mother didn't like him. Jason liked practical jokes and was usually fun to be around, although tonight's joke had been in poor taste, and she wasn't at all amused by it. As he stepped onto the pavement, he turned and gave her a small wave. Then he headed for home. She smiled and was about to turn to head back into the kitchen when a gloved hand grabbed her from behind. Her eyes widened, and fear returned as she opened her mouth to scream, but the intruder stepped closer and covered her mouth. An approaching train could be heard in the background.

"Don't scream. If he hears and comes running to your rescue, I'll kill him. Do you understand?"

Katie nodded as she fought back her tears. It seemed that her earlier premonition of seeing her face on a poster would come true after all.

"That's better. Now let's go. You'll make a fine playmate."

Chapter Two

Larry Davis, a man in his mid-twenties, dressed in hip, New York "GQ" style clothing, was a cub reporter for his hometown newspaper. Downing a shot of tequila, he meticulously aligned the glass in a row with four others. Several customers eyed Larry as he laid a $100 tip on the bar in the train station, making sure that he caught their glances. As soon as they looked away, he quickly switched it out with a single dollar bill and glanced at his watch. The train was scheduled to depart in three minutes.

Leaving the bar, he darted through the crowd at Penn Station, NY City's main train depot. Plowing past numerous nondescript people, he artfully maneuvered to the front of the ticket line. Coming face-to-face with the Ticket Lady, her hair and clothing, including a poodle skirt, bobby socks, and saddle shoes, were straight out of the fifties.

"Where to?" she asked with a deep smoker's rasp.

"Three first-class tickets to Atlanta," he replied as he removed a small stack of credit cards from his left front pants pocket. Shuffling through them, he pulled out one and handed it to her.

She swiped it and frowned. "Sorry, no good," she said sharply, extending the card toward him.

"Try it again," Larry said.

She did. "It's been denied."

"They're just dirty," he said.

He pulled another from the pile and wiped it against his sleeve before exchanging it for the one she held, but the result was the same.

"Worthless."

She handed it back to him. Her patience wasn't the only one growing thin.

"Come on, buddy," the guy in line behind him said. "Move it along."

Larry shuffled and pulled a third card from the stack. "I know this one is good," he said, holding it out to her.

"Are we playing cards or buying a ticket?" she asked as she traded the worthless one for his latest offering.

Larry knew by her expression that if this one did not go through, he would be asked to leave the line. "Just try it… Please?"

She swiped the new card. "This is your lucky day," she said, handing it back.

Putting away the cards, he was relieved until he noticed how slowly Ticket Lady was pecking away at the keys of her computer, using only one finger. Glancing at his watch, he saw that the train would now be leaving in less than two minutes.

"One finger? Come on, lady, at least use two fingers. It'll go twice as fast."

She raised her hand and flipped him off. "You mean this one?"

When she finally had the tickets ready, he snatched them from her hand. Turning, he hurried from the line toward his friends, twenty-two-year-old Quinn Blake, who was beautiful with short, curly blonde hair and mischievous blue eyes, and Jamal Ibori, a native African from Ghana in his early thirties, who stood a foot taller than everyone, wearing his "doorman's" uniform from work.

Larry held up the tickets. "First class, baby! You gotta love me."

Larry shoved through the crowd without remorse, Jamal and Quinn in tow. They walked through the gate and hurried down the sidewalk between several sets of tracks. As they approached the steps to the rail car, Larry stopped and looked around. Quinn was nowhere in sight. She had remained behind in the lobby to snap photos with her professional, digital, multi-lens camera.

Flipping the camera's mode to black and white, Quinn captured artistic pictures of lonely people: A janitor lamenting over his mop and bucket; a ticket lady who never looked at the passengers' faces; and a nervous executive with mismatched socks sitting in one of the plastic chairs, waiting for his train.

Quinn eyed a crippled old woman, struggling to put an empty ice tea bottle in a recycle bin. Unable to shoot the photo, Quinn felt paralyzed, unable to help. As she stood there, Larry swooped in and abruptly grabbed the bottle from the old lady, stuffing it into the bin for her. She smiled gratefully at him.

"Let's go, Quinn! We're gonna miss the wedding."

They rushed through the platform door at their gate and hurried along the walkway toward the waiting train. But now, Jamal was nowhere in sight. Hoping that he might have already gotten on board the train, the two friends rushed to the car. There they found Jamal, standing at attention in a swarm of people, politely helping some of the women and children up that first steep step and onto the train. At the same time, the conductor watched, clearly amused.

"Good morning. Have a nice trip. Good morning, Jamal said with a warm smile. "Good morning. Thank you."

Larry pulled him away. "Jamal, you're not at work! Let's go!"

Entering the train, they moved down the aisle of one car after another, passed already seated passengers, and others struggling to shove their suitcases onto the overhead rack. Four cars down, they finally found two sets of empty seats on either side of the aisle. Quinn shoved her case into the rack and slid into the seat next to the window on the right side of the aisle. Larry sat next to her, while Jamal took the outside seat across from them.

With slowly growing strength, the train crawled out of the station and into the early morning urban forest of concrete buildings in downtown New York.

* * *

Shaky Pete's Bar was lit with neon beer signs and bright lighting that hung over the pool tables. Strips of morning sunshine streaked through the blinds, cutting through stale, leftover cigarette smoke that still lingered in the air, even though the smokers had left the building hours earlier. Owner, bartender, and cook Shaky Pete was rotund, sweaty, and unshaven. He wore a stained white tank-top as he wiped off the top of the bar with a filthy rag.

Shadows fell on his only customer this morning, Sheriff Ron Packy, a worn and haggard man of forty. His dreams had been destroyed a few years earlier when he lost his wife and child in a tragic car accident. The lawman lifted a mug of beer and drained it.

"Give me another one, Pete," the Sheriff said as he slammed the mug down on the wooden surface. By the expression on his haggard and drawn face, this was not his first beer of the morning, and it probably wouldn't be his last. He looked terrible, barely holding up his head of dark brown hair with one hand.

"Can't, Sheriff, we're still closed," Pete said, hoping that Packy would take the hint and leave. "It's against the law."

"I *am* the law around here," Packy said.

"All the more reason to set a good example for others," Pete mumbled as he refilled the Sheriff's mug from the tap. Packy downed half the brew and let out a heavy smoker's wheeze. Other than Pete and Packy, the bar was empty except for the dishwasher, who, after drying the last of the once dirty glasses, started running the vacuum cleaner. The phone rang, which was odd, considering that the bar was closed, and Pete picked it up.

"Shaky, Pete's." The bartender listened to the distressed caller and then extended the receiver toward the Sheriff. "It's for you, Packy. Sounds important."

Taking the phone, Packy strained to hear over the sound of the loud vacuum. "Yeah? What? I can't hear you!"

"Turn it off, George!" Pete shouted.

George obeyed, and Packy straightened up, carefully listening to the woman frantically shouting in his ear. Pete rolled a cigarette and casually placed himself within earshot.

"Okay, Bernadette, tell me again," the Sheriff said now that he could actually hear the words that tumbled from her lips.

The woman's voice was so panicky and loud that Pete had no problem making out what she told the Sheriff.

"No, I didn't see her tonight," Packy said. "Sure, fine, relax. I'll come right over."

As the Sheriff punched the off button on the handset and set it down on the bar, Pete slyly moved aside.

"Woman problems?"

"You know I don't have a woman," Packy replied as he reached into his pocket and dropped a few wrinkled bills and coins onto the counter.

Leaving the last of his beer behind, he slammed open the front door and walked outside. The morning light blinded his eyes until he pulled a pair of sunglasses from his shirt pocket and slipped them on. Sheriff Packy's Police Jeep was parked near the door. It was floor littered with old cigarette butts and empty paper coffee cups. He climbed inside and started the engine. It sputtered and quit. Swearing under his breath, he popped the hood and tried to determine the trouble. As he tested wires and spark plugs, the police lights suddenly flashed, followed by a melting scream from the siren. Hillbilly bystanders offered no help, and shamefully shook their heads. A moment later, Barry Manilow music filled the air.

Clean-cut, always smiling, Deputy Dale Clark stroked his perfect mustache of thick chestnut hair. He sang to the tune as he drove up in a 1980 civilian car decorated with large car magnets imprinted: *Dobson Valley Sheriff's Department*. Dale's head popped up around Jeep, surprising his boss.

"Howdy-ho," Deputy Dale called. "Good morning, Sheriff. Havin' car trouble? How can I help?"

"Quit singing that shit, will ya?" Packy grumbled.

Dale ignored him and grabbed a stack of papers off the front seat of his vehicle. "I stayed up all night, printing off these photos of the girls. They came out real nice like," he said, handing the murder photos to the Sheriff.

"Fix my damn Jeep," Packy growled, ignoring the pictures.

The two men might as well have been on different planets. Neither seemed to pay the least bit of attention to what the other was saying.

"I've got more sizes at home!" Dale said, grinning.

Without another word, Packy snatched the photos from his Deputy's hand and took off in Dale's car.

Chapter Three

The wheels of the Amtrak clickety-clacked, breaking the early evening silence as it sped through the beautiful Appalachian countryside, snaking around the hills, mountains, and through tunnels. The sun's fading light was frequently stolen by the obstructions of the mountain terrain. Although the sky was cast in the half-light, darkness covered the ground as the train's whistle hauntingly echoed through the hills.

Larry Davis sat at one of the tables in the first-class dining car. Tapping away on his laptop keyboard and concentrating on the article, he was writing for his newspaper. Absentmindedly pushing a pair of wire-rimmed glasses higher on his nose as he thought about what he wanted to say next.

He wasn't alone at the table, and he looked up at his companions when a burst of laughter broke his concentration. Sitting across from him, Jamal's beaming smile reached all the way to his chocolate brown eyes. Built like a football player and very handsome, Jamal's medium brown skin glowed with health. Seated next to Larry was Quinn, who had a streetwise edge to her laugh. She and Jamal were just finishing their meal.

Larry raised an eyebrow. "Do you mind?"

Quinn continued to chuckle as Jamal turned to their friend.

"Come on, Larry. Why are you still working?"

"I need to finish this article for Sunday's Lifestyle section," Larry replied. "I won't enjoy the wedding until it's done and sent to the paper, Jamal."

"Story," Quinn said, shaking her head. "You see everyone's life as a possible story." Lifting her hands into the air, Quinn used her fingers to put quotation marks around the word "story."

"It's not about the article," Jamal interjected. "It's all about getting his father's approval."

"Thank you, Dr. Freud. I write about the stories I see," Larry said, defensively.

"Yes, but you don't see the *people* behind your stories," Quinn insisted. "Your writing is nothing more than a collection of words. You don't seem to understand that what you're creating isn't a story to the people you write about. It's their life."

"Thank you, Ann Landers," Larry replied, shrugging indifferently.

His response hurt Quinn's feelings. She wasn't trying to be critical. She simply wanted him to understand that his writing could be a lot more meaningful if he would only dig deeper into the heart of the people involved.

The waitress laid the check on the table. As Quinn and Jamal divided the amount in three, Larry stole the bill.

"Oh no, you don't," Larry said. "I've got it."

"That's too much," Jamal said. "We'll split the bill."

Larry ignored him and turned to Quinn. "If you let me see your photos, we'll split it."

"Fine," she replied, handing him her camera.

"Not the ones you just took. I want to see the book," Larry said.

She saw the guys grin at each other and realized that they had a conspiracy going.

"Whatever. They're not that good," she said. "The printer never gets the pictures quite right."

"The book..." Jamal said.

17

She dug into her bag and pulled out a nicely bound photo album. Jamal studied it, while Larry looked on.

"They're black and white," Larry exclaimed, uncertain as to why anyone would choose to take pictures in what he considered to be an old style. "Why not in color?"

"Like I said before, you don't understand, Larry," Quinn said. "Black and white photos connect with people on an emotional level. It shows things that would otherwise be lost in a color shot."

"Unlike your stories," Jamal added, "these aren't just images of people. Quinn captures their essence…their very soul."

"It's your photos," Larry said. "Anyway, your photography is a perfect excuse for our train excursion through the Appalachians before meeting the others in Atlanta."

Quinn eyed Larry suspiciously. "As opposed to flying? And here I thought it was to save money on the fare."

"How much money did you make?" Larry asked her.

She grabbed the book away from him in disgust. "You just don't get it, do you? This is why you're no longer my boyfriend, and by the way, you can pay the tab."

"Excuse me, but I broke up with you," Larry said as he slipped a $100 tip on the table for the others to see. It was the same $100 bill he had used in the train station bar.

Jamal shook his head in wonder. "I don't know how you do it."

"I do quite well financially," Larry assured him.

"No," Jamal said. "I don't know how the two of you remain friends."

They stood up and exited the dining car. As they went through the door and entered the noisy space where one train car connected to the next, Larry stopped.

"Hold on," he said. "I forgot my cell phone. Go on ahead. I'll catch up."

Larry hurried back just in time to see the waitress pocket her $100.00 tip.

"Pardon me. I'm sorry. I think I got my money mixed up," he told her, snatching the $100.00 bill from her pocket and handing her a few dollars in exchange. He was totally oblivious of her look of disappointment.

* * *

Inside the Cape Cod house, where Katie had been kidnapped, ominous shadows fled as early morning sunlight poured through the kitchen window, lighting the room. A flashlight beam revealed a missing fuse – the one that provided power to the lights in the living room and kitchen.

Katie's mother, Bernadette, still wore the clothing she had donned last evening for a night on the town. Still, her makeup was blotchy from crying, and her mascara had smeared and run down her cheeks. The same age as Packy, she'd had her daughter out of wedlock at the age of eighteen. Her coloring was the same as Katie's, and her figure was still slender and softy curving. She watched as Sheriff Packy studied the empty fuse socket in the tiny dark closet space."

"Yep," the Sheriff said, "just what I figured. It's the fuse."

Bernadette handed him a new one, and he screwed it in. The lights came on, revealing their closeness.

"Where were you last night?" Packy asked.

"I went out. Something you and I never did when we dated," she replied.

19

The Sheriff squeezed past her and stepped into the kitchen, putting his head under the faucet and running cold water over his face to sober up. When he straightened up, he took a difficult look at his reflection in the kitchen window and did not like what he saw.

"Why didn't your date fix it?"

Agitated, Bernadette studied him a moment before replying, "he dropped me off at the end of the driveway."

"Someday, your date might actually walk you to the door," Packy said sarcastically as he dried his face and head with a paper towel. Tossing it in the wastebasket, he noticed a broken fuse lying on the floor. As he stared at it, his mind imagined a hand removing the fuse and smashing it with the heel of his booted foot. Returning to reality, he inconspicuously picked up the broken fuse, dropped it into his pocket, and covertly scoured the room for more clues. Bernadette contemptuously eyed Packy, barely resisting the urge to chide him about his hangover.

"What were Katie's plans last night?"

"She told me she was coming right home after work," Bernadette replied. "You know her. She'd do exactly that. But when I checked her room, I realized that she hadn't slept in her bed."

"She probably met up with her boyfriend," Packy said. "What's his name…Jason?"

"My daughter doesn't have a boyfriend, and if she did, he wouldn't dare step inside this house, especially when I'm not here. I'd kill them both. Besides, she would never leave without her purse."

"Her purse is here?" Packy asked.

"Yes, I found it here on the counter," she said, pointing to a spot near the sink. "Right next to the note, I had left telling her where I was."

Packy spotted a handmade cigarette barely sticking out from under the bottom edge of the fridge. The image sent his mind back to the bar, and he mentally watched as Pete rolled a cigarette. He imagined a flick and turned in the direction of the projected cigarette toss. Then he eyed the back door.

"Does Bart smoke?"

"No," Bernadette replied.

"Been going out with any other men?"

Bernadette narrowed her eyes. "Why are you acting like you suddenly care about my life and who I date?"

"I do care about your life...and your daughter's, too."

"Is this about my dating or Katie not coming home? Because if you think you could run my life, you got another thing."

Sheriff Packy imagined muddy work boots leaving tracks across the kitchen floor. "Did Bart wear work boots on your date? You didn't happen to be trampling around in the woods last night, were you?"

"No. Again, that is something only you managed to do. Why are you asking me all these questions? You're scaring me, Packy. I know you. Something's wrong...terribly wrong. Is she the latest victim?" She stepped closer and grabbed the front of his shirt, shaking him. "Tell me!"

The Sheriff looked up, pretending confusion. "What are you talking about?"

"I didn't ask you here to fix my damn fuse box. *Katie's missing!"* She said, giving him an incredulous look.

"Calm down, easy now. Talk to me."

"I've been defending you to the whole town for the past six months, telling them about what a good cop you are and how you would find the monster who is murdering our young women. But now, my daughter is missing, just like Teresa Crawford's girl! Do you hear me? My *daughter* is the latest victim! That's the only plausible explanation."

"Now, Bernadette, as far as we know, she has run off with some boy and is living it up in New York or some other big city," he said, gently stroking her hair.

She pushed away from his caress. "Is that what you tell all the parents before you find their daughters' mutilated bodies?"

"You're jumping to conclusions, especially with a young daughter who probably just stayed out all night with her boyfriend."

"*Katie doesn't have a boyfriend*!" Bernadette screeched. Now that she had spoken the words out loud, she desperately tried to keep herself from becoming hysterical, but it was a losing battle. "Stay out of the bar and find her!"

Sheriff Packy's radio crackled.

"Sheriff Packy, do you copy?" The Deputy's voice came through loud and clear. "We have a..."

"Not now." Packy turned off the radio, but Bernadette eyed him suspiciously. She had a pretty good idea of what Dale was about to say.

Chapter Four

Dirty, sweaty, and shoeless, Katie huddled in the corner of a nondescript, dimly lit room with wooden walls. Tears streamed down her face, which was already read and blotchy from crying all night. Her hair was wild and matted as she struggled against the ropes binding her wrists, causing angry red rope burns and some mild bleeding.

"Please, please let me out," she begged. "Let me go home... Please! I know you're watching me. Let me out!"

Since she was gagged, her words were muffled. She tried to sit up from her position but awkwardly tumbled back against the chair. Her fear and frustration increased, and she cried out. "Mom! Help me. Get me out of here."

No one heard her, however, but the person behind the eye that watched through a peephole. Just watching, creeping Katie out even more...

* * *

Outside in the town of Dobson Valley, an old fire truck, a rescue squad vehicle, and an array of pickup trucks fitted with makeshift flashing lights lined a seldom-used dirt road deep in a heavily forested part outside of town. The Sheriff pulled up and parked his car next to the fire truck. Methodically, he collected a pair of disposable gloves and a kit filled with specialized investigative tools from the trunk of his car. As he approached the edge of the incline, he eyed the congregation of tobacco-spitting volunteer firefighters standing in a group below.

Slipping and sliding down the slope, he descended to the creek and the crime scene on the bank beside it. Barry Manilow music filled the air as Deputy Dale cheerfully sang along while stepping over a girl's body, which was dressed in a doll-like costume and lying face down in the water. Even the birds and insects seemed a bit disrespectful as they gaily chirped and twittered to the music. Flashes of light cut through the shady area as Deputy Dale took still photos of the victim that, even to the untrained eye, looked more provocative than investigative.

At the sound of the Sheriff's approach, he looked up and grinned. "Howdy-do, Sheriff!"

Packy gave him a sour look. In his mind, it just wasn't right to be so cheerful while working such a grisly scene.

"Good news. I got the Jeep fixed," the Deputy said, ignoring the expression on his boss's face. "What do you think we have here?"

"You're an idiot, Dale. What do you think we have here? Why don't you step on the other side of the victim and mess up more evidence while you are at it?" Packy barked.

"Now, why would I want to go and do that?" Dale replied. He seemed totally clueless as to why Packy was angry at him.

"Exactly, now get the hell away from there. Yer always screwing up the crime scene and destroying the evidence. And why is that music playing? Have you no respect for the dead?"

"I thought it would help brighten everyone's spirits."

"Turn that shit off! The only thing that's going to brighten anyone's spirits is catching the bastard that did this to her and the other victims."

As soon as Dale stepped back from the crime scene, the Sheriff inspected the area with the deftness the seasoned FBI agent he had once been, but that had been another time in what seemed like an entirely different lifetime – his life before...

No, I can't think about that now. As he worked, the esteemed Mayor, Patrick Farlow approached, careful not to get too close. Rotund and a Southern sophisticate, he wore new clothes at least a decade out of date. Still, they were the latest craze in the local general store. The mayor wanted to present the best possible image to his constituents.

"I sure hope it's not Katie," Mayor Farlow said.

Startled, Sheriff Packy turned to him. "Howdy, Mayor." Lowering his voice to barely a whisper, he asked, "how'd you know about Katie? I haven't said a word to anyone yet."

"Uh...Bernadette called looking for you," the Mayor replied. He lowered his voice to barely above a whisper. "Is this one any different from the others?"

"I'm afraid not," Packy replied, shaking his head in despair. "She's barefoot, her hair has been braided into pigtails, her nails have been manicured, and she's dressed up like a little girl. The body was dumped in the creek, possibly to destroy evidence."

Packy's mind drifted, and he imagined the terrified girl being forcibly dressed and having her hair brushed by a shadowy figure. Then he saw her dead body being dragged through woods and eventually dumped into the slow running stream. A nondescript hand hesitated just a moment before removing the girl's shoes. A moment later, his mind was brought back to reality when a car wildly screeched to a stop on the road above. Bernadette jumped from her vehicle, leaving the door open as she slid, tripped, and picked her way down the slope, her eyes wild with fear of what she would discover below.

"I'm guessing that the facial make-up is the same and the eyes have been punched out," Packy told the mayor, after gently turning the body over and examining it.

When Bernadette arrived, she swallowed and took a deep breath before peering over Packy's shoulder to see the victim's face with the make-up smeared and the girl's eyes missing. Bernadette froze and then fell to her knees, vomiting and wracked with tears. The entire posse of rescue workers stopped what they were doing and looked on as Packy pulled her to her feet and held her, whispering soothing words to try and calm her down.

"Talk about messin' up yer crime scene," Dale began, but shut up when Packy threw him a dirty look.

"Damn it! It's Teresa Crawford," Packy growled. "She's only been missing a week. It looks like the killer has picked up the pace. The last girl had been missing nearly a month before her body was found."

"What does that tell you, Sheriff?" Mayor Farlow asked.

"I don't know. Each new body sends me down a rabbit hole. I don't get it. This murderer is evolving. The girls are still dressed in doll's costumes and left in the creek to destroy any evidence that might have helped us. The eyes are punched out like an old doll's face that has had its shoe button eyes plucked out, and all of them have been dumped without their shoes. After that, it changes."

"It all looks the same to me," the Mayor sadly replied.

26

"No. Look here. The ankles and wrists have fresh rope burns. The others were partially healed. Remember?"

"Hmmm," the Mayor said thoughtfully. "I never would've realized that."

Packy broke his embrace and shouted. "Dale! Escort Bernadette to her car and make sure she gets home safely."

Dale nodded. As he led the distraught woman to his car, he took advantage of her distress, secretly stealing touches on her body that went far beyond what a friend would do. When he reached his vehicle, she slapped his face.

"Don't ever touch me again."

Back at the crime scene, the Sheriff and the Mayor continued their conversation.

"There is one thing different this time, though," the Sheriff said. "After she was murdered and dumped, she was cut postmortem with the skill of a butcher. That's never good, and it hasn't happened before."

"Was she sexually abused?" Mayor Farlow asked.

"We'll have to wait until the doc examines her. If she was, I'm bettin' there's no trace of semen, just like the others."

"I'm telling you, Packy. This is one perverted son-of-a-bitch."

"Let's hope that with the perp ratcheting upping the stakes, he'll have slipped up and left some forensic evidence behind."

"I hope for both our sakes that he has," the Mayor said. "Don't get me wrong, Packy. I think you're doing a great job, but I don't believe you're gettin' anywhere fast on this one. People are scared, and I'm under a great deal of pressure here."

"Look, Mayor, anywhere else I'd have a task force assembled with police, deputies, FBI, you name it. We would get a lot farther a lot quicker if I had a team to work with. Here I have to do everything myself."

"You want to call in the FBI?" Mayor Farlow asked. He was surprised and not a little uncomfortable about the idea of outside law enforcement overrunning his town. There were things happening here that outsiders might not understand. "What about Dale?"

"What about him? He's little more than a backwoods hick. No offense, Mayor. He's always bumbling around, messing up the crime scene and destroying possible evidence," Packy said, disgusted. "And then there's his…odd sense of crime scene photos. I swear. He acts more like a photographer for some girlie magazine than a deputy."

"What about doc? Surely he gives you the information you need."

Packy shook his head sadly. "Doc Abernathy is just a smalltime country doctor. He's good enough to take care of folks and their animals around here, but he doesn't have the necessary training to be a proper coroner and doesn't know what to look for when it comes to forensic evidence, not like a true forensics expert. If I had any sense, I'd at least send the bodies over to county."

"Now, Packy, you know that folks 'round here wouldn't stand for a bunch of strangers messing around with their daughters' remains," the Mayor warned. "They're unhappy enough about the autopsies."

"Damnit, I know that. But it's the law. Murder victims have to be autopsied. The way things are going, it's either going to come down to bringing in outside help, or we may have to face the fact that we might never catch this monster. I'm this close…," he held up his right thumb and forefinger about a quarter of an inch apart. "…to assembling a task force before this pervert kidnaps yet another victim."

"Before we do that," the Mayor urged. "I think it's time to tell me everything you know so far. I want to make sure that we have no other options available to us before I allow a bunch of big-city strangers to come tromping through my town and upsetting everyone."

Packy turned to him, but his eyes were fixed on the victim's body. He was upset over the Mayor's decision. He couldn't understand why he was so hesitant to allow others to help with the case. It just didn't make any sense, especially with the body count still rising.

"You want a profile? Well, here it is, Patrick. There's something random about this killer and the way he operates. Aside from age and being pretty, none of the victims have anything in common. The perp is most likely a white male. He's most likely from a low to middle-class background and is somewhere between his late twenties to middle thirties…could be as old as forty. He would have a difficult time keeping a steady job, and when he does work, he's probably doing manual labor. He most likely had a domineering mother or was abandoned by his father at an early age. I suspect that he doesn't have a social connection to women and probably doesn't date. Maybe the perp's behavior turns girls off, or possibly his presence makes others uncomfortable. The suspect doesn't have much control over his own life, so he compensates by exerting control over his victims. What's worse…I believe it's one of our own. Someone we know and see all the time."

As he recited the profile of the perp, Sheriff Packy pictured in his mind a shadowy figure spying on young women from a distance and gawking as they walked past. He then imagined the killer dragging a screaming girl across the dirt and later tying her up in a basement below a low wattage hanging light. He mentally closed the scene before his mind could show him the terrible things that he knew were being done to these women.

Packy's vision dissolved. He and the Mayor looked around at the crowd that had begun to gather.

"I hate to say it, but that profile could fit any number of people," the Mayor said, keeping his voice pitched low.

The men stared at each other, their minds picturing alleged suspects. In the background, Dale snuck another provocative photo of the corpse, drawing the Sheriff's attention. Then Packy spotted mud on the Deputy's shoes…mud that did not match the crime scene. His next thought made his blood run cold. Could his own deputy be the one murdering these women, even though he didn't completely fit the profile? No way... Still, he couldn't totally discount the idea, and that bothered him more than he cared to admit, even to himself.

Another flash went off, as Dale continued taking pictures, and Packy's suspicions grew even stronger. A moment later, Doc Abernathy pulled up in his 1957 Chevy station wagon.

* * *

Quinn's flash burst as she took an artistic image of an elderly couple asleep in their seat, holding hands. Seeing no other interesting shots, she looked around for her friends and called out softly so as not to wake senior citizens.

"Larry? Jamal?"

They were nowhere to be seen as the train sped through the Appalachians, passing through more wilderness than small towns. Log cabins dotted the countryside here, and there were old rusted cars from the '40s and '50s parked helter-skelter across the lawns. Other rusted equipment such as tools, old kitchen appliances, and plows also littered the properties. The passengers on the train would occasionally see a farmer plowing his fields, and in one town, two old-timers sat on the porch in front of a hardware store, playing their banjos while a couple of kids laughed and screamed as they chased a squealing piglet.

As the train passed deeper into the mountains, the scenes became even odder – at least to the eyes of someone from the big city. Larry sat alone in the café car, unknowingly coordinating a shot of vodka with each new mountain shack they passed. After this last drink, he felt the first twinge of drunkenness – a buzzing sensation between his eyes, and he wondered if he should stop before he got any drunker. Spotting another wooden shingled house in the distance, his mind drifted to another place, another time, and as the train drew closer to the rundown building, he pictured himself as a small boy sitting on the porch, watching the train pass. Larry shook his head and looked again, the image of himself as a boy was no longer there, and he quickly downed another shot.

Flash!

Larry's head jerked up as Quinn snapped a sharply focused, artistic black and white image of him sitting next to the window, blurring the background.

Larry looked at her. "Why'd you do that?"

Quinn smiled. "I captured a part of you."

"What…a guy looking out the window?" He asked, puzzled.

"Nope," she replied as she dropped down onto the bench seat across from him. "Tell me what you were thinking, and I'll tell you what I saw."

"I was just watching the scenery."

"No you weren't," Quinn said. "You were deep in thought about something, possibly something from your past?"

"What makes you think that?"

"The camera never lies."

"Then ask your camera, not me," Larry grumbled as he resumed watching the mountain farmhouses fly past. He had never told anyone about his wretched childhood, and he wasn't about to start now.

* * *

Back in Dobson Valley, the Crawford home was similar to the mountain houses seen from the passing train, with chickens running free on a dirt lawn. Mr. Crawford chopped firewood, while his young daughter, Scout, watched as she sat on an old tree stump. After splitting a log and tossing the pieces onto a growing pile near the house, he grabbed the next log and set it up on a tree stump. Raising the ax, he was about to swing the sharp blade downward, when he spotted a ghostly cloud of dust following the Sheriff's Jeep as it climbed the dirt road leading to the house. Crawford stopped in mid-swing but did not drop the ax.

"Git inside and fetch your momma," he told his daughter.

"Why, Daddy?"

"Do as I tell ya," Crawford said firmly, his gruffly spoken words frightening the child just a little.

As he finished speaking, Mrs. Crawford came to the door and eyed the approaching Sheriff's car, fear and dread filling her heart. "Scout! Git in here!"

"Aw, Mama, I want to see the Sheriff's car," she whined, dragging her feet as she headed for the front door.

Mrs. Crawford shoved her daughter into the house just as Packy pulled up and got out of his Jeep. Fear was plain on her face as she hurried over to her husband. Both seemed to know that the news they were about to hear would confirm their worst nightmares. He dropped the ax and placed his arm around her, giving her a comforting squeeze. Packy remained by his vehicle and touched the brim of his hat. But before he could say anything, Mr. Crawford, his expression grim, spoke first.

"Ya found her, didn't ya?"

Packy closed the distance between them and touched Mrs. Crawford's shoulder. "I'm sorry. I'm so very sorry for your loss."

"We had a feeling she was with the Lord," Mrs. Crawford said, tears spilling down her cheeks. "She was a strong believer, and I know she's where no one else can ever hurt her again."

Crawford stepped forward away from his wife. "You son-of-a-bitch, it was your job to find her *alive*! But you didn't, and now she's dead. I hope the image of her body stays with you for the rest of your life. I hope you see her face every night in your nightmares, along with the faces of all the other poor girls that have lost their lives to this monster."

"It's not his fault," Mrs. Crawford said, moving forward and gripping her husband's arm.

"You were an FBI failure in Chicago. Now you're a small-town Sheriff, and you're still a failure here. Why did you even come back? You should have stayed in Chicago, and I should've voted for the other guy. Maybe he would have been able to find this killer in time, and my daughter would still be alive." Mr. Crawford took a deep breath. "I don't know what I expected. You couldn't even save your own wife and child."

His words shook Packy and took him back in time to a place he saw all too often in his dreams, a place he wished he could forget.

* * *

A *younger Sheriff Packy approached a roadside traffic accident, consisting of a mound of steaming crumpled metal that used to be his wife's car. A second vehicle with a crumpled front end had plowed into the back and shoved the trunk all the way to the back seat, instantly killing his daughter. His wife had also died at the scene several minutes later. The second car's passenger remained inside his vehicle, too drunk to completely comprehend the horrible thing he had done. He had a small bloody injury to his forehead from hitting the steering wheel but was otherwise unhurt.*

* * *

Packy shook his head to clear the unwanted memory.

"It's okay. I understand," the Sheriff said sadly.

He was about to step back when Mr. Crawford slugged him in the face with a large, meaty fist and grabbed him by the collar, pushing him back against the Jeep.

"Stop it, Buford!" Mrs. Crawford screamed. "You want to end up in jail for assaultin' the Sheriff? This isn't going to bring our baby back to us."

"You'll never understand what we're feelin'. To have one of your own blood taken away," Crawford shouted at Packy. "You know damn well that sleazeball Shaky Pete did it. Him and that scum what hangs around his bar. Have you even bothered to check his place above the bar for evidence? Get off the bottle n' do somethin' right for a change!"

The Sheriff shoved Crawford back and grabbed his upper arm, fist cocked, ready for a punch. "I *am* doing something, and I do understand how it feels. Both my daughter and my wife were taken away. It's *you* who will never understand what I'm feelin'." The Sheriff drew his fist back further, but instead of punching the grief-stricken man, he dropped his arm and shoved him back a step. "Mrs. Crawford, Mr. Crawford…, I'm sorry. But I need to retake a look around her room."

Mr. Crawford turned away in disgust, too overcome to say anything more, but his wife gave the Sheriff a nod. Packy entered the house, brushing past Scout, who stared at him, her eyes wide with shock and filled with unshed tears. She was too young to completely understand what had just happened, but she knew it was something bad and that it involved her older sister.

"She's never coming back, is she?" The little girl asked.

Packy slowly shook his head and walked past her toward her sister's bedroom. Theresa's room was decorated in North Carolina Cornflower Blue. A stuffed Ram's head mascot rested against the center of the bed pillows, just as she had left it the morning she had disappeared. In fact, the room had not been disturbed, looking as though she had just stepped out moments earlier. As the Sheriff scanned the room, he heard the sound of firewood being split once more. He didn't really expect to find anything new. The girl hadn't owned a computer, so it was unlikely that her killer had located her electronically. In his initial search shortly after she had disappeared, he had found a diary Teresa had kept. But after thoroughly examining it, he had found nothing more than the usual ramblings of a teenage girl about her boyfriend, school, friends, etc. The boy was a local, who checked out and had a solid alibi for the time of her disappearance.

Giving the room one last sweep, Packy touched a figurine of an angel that had the tip broken off one wing. As he did, his mind flashed back, and he imagined Teresa's pretty face. He could picture her sneaking out through her bedroom window after dark, wearing newly purchased red shoes. Her waiting father, however, had caught and dragged her back to her room where an argument and a struggle ensued, ending with the figurine being accidentally broken. *Too bad he hadn't caught her that night. She might still be alive.* His mind returned to the present when Mrs. Crawford entered the room and touched his arm.

"I'm sorry…about Buford hittin' you and all. He doesn't mean those hurtful things he said to you. We're just torn up about our girl… And you…I'm sorry. We had no idea."

"I know. I know," Packy assured her. "This has been going on for so long that I've come to expect this sort of reaction. Can't be helped, I guess. Folks around here are scared, fearing that their daughter may be next."

"All she ever wanted was to go to Carolina…North Carolina State. She was so excited. She even won a scholarship that would have paid for her schooling and all. It would have been difficult to come up with the money for room and board, but we'd have managed somehow." She gazed around the room, picturing her daughter there and soaking up every shred of memory she could. "Everything was Cornflower Blue... That's their color, you know...the school. Funny thing, she would only wear red high heels when she went out. It makes you wonder why."

"Hmm," Packy said, scratching his chin. "Seems like a conflict of interest, wearing a rival's color."

His response seemed to startle her, and her mind went blank. When her eyes refocused, she said, "I think the red shoes were more about the boys. We didn't care for her dressing sexy and all. Attracts too much of the wrong kind of attention if you ask me. But that's what she had on when she disappeared." She paused a moment. "I guess we were right. It seems they did attract the wrong kind of attention. Yet the funny thing is that I miss seeing those shoes sitting next to her dresser here in her room. They were so much a part of her that them bein' gone just makes her loss feel more...real."

"We found one shoe at the crime scene. I'm sorry, but I have to hang on to it as evidence," Packy said.

"Only one?" Mrs. Crawford asked. "I wonder what happened to the other one. I sure would like to have them back...sort of a memorial to Teresa."

"I promise. I'll find the other shoe, and after her killer is brought to justice, I'll return them both so that you can have them as a remembrance. Chances are the killer kept one shoe as a trophy," Packy said, causing Mrs. Crawford to shiver. He turned to leave the room but stopped. "You can claim the body in a couple of days at Clifford's Funeral

Home, as soon as the Doc finishes the autopsy. Again, I'm very sorry for your loss. I wish…I wish I could have found her in time. I'm sorry."

He stepped into the hallway, but Mrs. Crawford stopped him.

"Sheriff, I hope you don't mind if I pray for you and that the good Lord will help you catch this monster."

"Thanks," Packy replied. "I need all the help I can get."

Chapter Five

The train slowed down as it pulled into a small town depot consisting of a small wooden platform with a roof overhead to keep passengers dry on rainy or snowy days and nothing else. No one got on the train at this stop. There was no building close by where a ticket could be purchased. Instead, they were sold at one of the small establishments in town, probably at the local drug store. But a couple passengers did depart here while others left the train to stretch their legs and grab a quick smoke.

In the club car, Larry, who had decided to continue drinking, drained another shot and bolted down the aisle for the car with the only open door and some air. Stretching his legs, he caught his breath and looked around, but was soon bored with the nondescript scenery. Spotting a wooden bench, he walked over and sat down, and as he stared at nothing in particular. His mind flashed back to a weathered mountain shack and his last memory of his mother.

* * *

A visitor had arrived, and Larry had been locked outside by his mother. Looking through the shack window, he saw her with the rich stranger he had seen before but had never been introduced to. As usual, the man-made sexual advances, and his mother did not resist. This affair had been going on for the past several years. Furious, Larry pushed against the secured door, but the two lovers did not hear him.

"Kiss me," the rich man said.

She kissed him passionately. "Leave your wife, and we'll be together forever," she whispered in a husky voice.

"No," he replied.

"Please. I've waited for so many years. The boy isn't getting any younger."

"I can't, and I won't!" He snarled.

Larry's mother stepped out of his embrace, her face red with anger. "If you don't, I'll tell the town that Larry is your son. You owe him a good life. You owe us a good life!"

Hearing the shouting inside, Larry ran to the front window and pressed his nose against the glass to see what was going on. As he did, he watched the nightmare scene unfold in frozen helplessness. Angry beyond reason over the threat, the man's sexual passion turned to violence. He grabbed Larry's mother by the hair and dragged her across the floor. Larry screamed as his mother fought back with everything she had. The struggle lasted for several moments. Then, breaking free, she headed for the door and burst out of the shack.

"Run, hide!" She shouted to her son as she ran across the tracks. Even though the rich man was the boy's father, she feared he would also be killed to hide the man's shame.

Larry hesitated until the man came outside, carrying a 9mm handgun. Seeing the boy, he took aim, his shot embedding into a nearby oak tree as Larry ran around the corner of the shack and headed for the woods. Taking off after the woman, the rich man fired a shot, and she dropped like a heavy sack of grain. The sound brought her son to a screeching halt, and as he turned around, he saw the man fire another round into his mother's head. Sobbing in fear and anguish, Larry took off again, knowing that if he was caught, especially after witnessing his mother's murder, he would be killed as well. Even though the man had shot at him before, he might not have bothered to chase after him, but not now.

* * *

As his mind returned to the present, Quinn stepped off the train and walked over to where he sat. Larry briefly glanced at her before nervously lighting a cigarette.

"What's wrong?" She asked.

"How come you didn't take a photo?"

"I don't need to," Quinn replied.

Larry looked down, not meeting her eyes. She seemed to know when he had drifted back to his past on the train and was afraid she might once more realize that he was experiencing an unpleasant flashback from the past.

"I just needed some fresh air."

Quinn stepped closer and lifted his chin. Realizing that he had been drinking too much, she didn't hide the disgusted look she had on her face. She could not understand why Larry drank so much.

"I'm sure that's helping," she said at last.

"You'd be surprised."

Jamal leaned out one of a train's windows. "All aboard!"

A moment later, he stood at attention by the open train door, waiting for the passengers to climb aboard and return to their seats. Larry and Quinn hurried over and climbed up the steps.

"Why do you do this, Jamal?" Larry asked. "You're not even getting paid."

"It makes me feel good," Jamal replied with a grin.

"Yeah, yeah, yeah, but you're not getting paid," Larry insisted. "You're just lucky the real conductors don't mind."

Ignoring Larry, Jamal quickly helped an elderly passenger up the steps.

"Why, thank you, young man," the woman said, slipping him a generous tip.

Jamal smiled, gloating just a little as he followed his friends inside so that the conductor could close and lock the train door. Larry hurried down the aisle, stopping in front of the restroom doors. There was one on each side of the aisle near the back of the car. Both were occupied, so he turned and walked through several cars before finding another one with a restroom.

"I'll catch up," he called to Jamal and Quinn. "Gotta take care of some business if you know what I mean."

When he reached the next pair of restrooms, he saw that the occupied sign showed that someone was inside. Looking at the opposite door, it appeared to be empty, so he reached for the handle and opened it. When he did, however, he found a teenager named Jimmy inside the cramped room, trying to light a joint. Wearing a guilty look, the kid jumped up from his seat on the toilet and dropped the lighter as well as a joint into the tiny metal sink on his left.

"Are you going to turn me in?" Jimmy nervously asked. Sweat started to trickle down his temple.

"No, kid, everything's cool. Sit down." Larry had to practically climb on top of Jimmy to squeeze inside and shut the door. "Where are you from...New York? Where ya headed?"

"Bryson City."

"Do you know what they would do to you in Appalachia if they caught you smoking that?"

"No," Jimmy replied as he nervously fished his joint and lighter out of the sink.

"Ever see the movie *Deliverance*? You know…," Larry paused for dramatic effect. "Can you squeal like a pig?"

Jimmy gulped. "That's just a movie. They wouldn't really… I mean…would they?"

Larry cooly nodded his head. "I know these people and what they're capable of. Believe me. It's not pretty. They're pretty crazy around these parts."

Jimmy looked at his watch. "Hey, I gotta get going. My mom's waiting for me," he said as he tried to squeeze past Larry to open the door and make his getaway.

"Hey, kid. I think its better if you don't take your temptation with you. Oink, oink."

"Yeah, …right."

Jimmy eagerly passed him the joint, then digging into his pockets, pulled out a few more. Pocketing them, Larry grinned at his good fortune and opened the door, · allowing the kid to leave, then he went back inside and sat down. Lighting the joint, he inhaled deeply, enjoying it thoroughly.

* * *

At Shaky Pete's establishment, Pete re-entered the building through the back door. The volume of the music from the jukebox increased as he moved behind the bar with its shelves of bottled liquor and wiped his hands on a rag. Nervous, he put the rag down and then picked it up twice more. Looking up, he realized that in his brief absence, Sheriff Packy had returned and was watching his every move with a critical eye.

"Hey, Sheriff," Pete called out, his voice almost too friendly. Was it his nerves?

"You okay, Pete?" The Sheriff asked.

"Ah sure. Of course. Why?"

That's the third time you've washed your hands in the past thirty seconds. Are they just dirty? Or are you tryin' to remove something that's no longer there…at least physically?"

Pete quickly dropped the rag, and nervously rolled a cigarette. "I have no idea what you mean. I just like being clean."

"You should change your shirt then," Packy said. "It looks like it hasn't been washed since Moses parted the red sea."

"What can I get you…a freebie?" Pete asked, hoping to take the sheriff's mind off whatever he was thinking about.

Packy, however, didn't look like he was in the mood for a drink. Instead, he seemed to take great interest in the hand-rolled cigarette that Pete prepared. "I thought you smoked Camels."

"Just started rolling." He looked up. "Why do you care?"

Pete looked away from the Sheriff, relieved when he heard a customer calling him from further down the bar.

"Hey! I need another drink down here!" Clyde called.

"Hold yer britches on, Clyde. I'm coming."

Moving under the watchful gaze of Packy, who was still sizing him up, Pete poured a double shot of whiskey. Filled a large glass with beer from the tap and took the boilermaker to the opposite end of the bar where Clyde Gilmore sat with a couple pals. Clyde was a real sleazeball who looked like he hadn't taken a bath in days. He chewed tobacco and carried a spit cup wherever he went, which he used fairly often. Packy nodded at him.

"Afternoon, Clyde."

Clyde spat into his cup and looked over at the sheriff. By the expression on his face, it was clear that he didn't really care for the lawman.

"Hard at it, Packy?"

"Couldn't say that I am," the Sheriff replied. "Off duty."

"Funny, we can't tell the difference anymore."

During this time, Packy casually examined the man from head to toe, when his gaze reached Clyde's boots, he noticed fresh mud caked on them. *Is that mud from down by the creek bed? I don't remember him being down there earlier.* Rubbing the back of his neck, Packy looked up at Clyde, his suspicions aroused.

Feeling the Sheriff's gaze, Clyde, who had turned away to down his shot, gave him a hostile look. "You gonna harass me now? I call it what it is, Sheriff. I don't care if you are a lawman. Yer a drunk! No doubt about it."

"Didn't see you earlier," Packy commented, ignoring Clyde's cantankerous remarks. "You got mud on your shoes. Puttin' in a little overtime?"

"Not that it's any of yer business, but I had some stuff to do," Clyde replied.

"Yeah? Doing some digging?" The Sheriff asked. "Whereabouts?"

45

A confused expression crossed Clyde's face until he realized that Packy was looking at his muddy boots. His irritated look changed to one of suspicion over Packy's comments. "Maybe. What's it to ya?"

"Everything's my business now," Packy replied.

Clyde's voice could not hide his growing aggression. "Take it somewhere else, Sheriff. I ain't done nothin', and you can't pin nothin' on me, cause I ain't done nothin'!"

Packy had heard it all before, and he was really tired of the dirty man's hostility. The more he thought about Clyde, the more the man seemed to fit the profile he had given to the Mayor earlier. He closed the distance between them and grabbed Clyde by the collar, throwing him against the bar.

"I'll decide if you ain't done nothin' and whether or not I think you've done somethin'. You got that? I'm the sheriff!"

"Then why don't you give our women folk a break. Folks 'round here are tired of worrying if their daughter might be the next victim. Find that killer, Mr. Sheriff, and stop accusin' innocent folks of doin' stuff they ain't done."

"Could be I'm holdin' the killer right now," Packy snarled.

"You're out of yer mind! I ain't touched them girls!"

"Prove it," Packy shot back.

"That's your job. You want to arrest me? Go right ahead, but I ain't done nothin'."

* * *

Still in his uniform, Deputy Clark walked across the tiled floor in his kitchen to a cabinet where he kept a bottle of maple syrup. Seeing that the container was nearly empty, he made a mental note to purchase more the next time he visited the local convenience store. Taking the bottle to the kitchen table, he poured the remaining syrup over a huge stack of buttermilk pancakes he had just cooked and dug in with relish. As he forked a bite into his mouth, a muffled whimper sounded from the floor above. Dale looked up, giving the ceiling a slow, disapproving grimace as he chewed. *I'll get to you pretty soon,* he thought.

In a dark wooden room, a girl struggled with her bonds, concentrating on working loose the knot that held her captive. Dried blood was caked on her wrists and lower arms where the ropes had cut into her tender skin. Still, she worked through the pain, pulling at her bonds with her teeth and clawing at the knot with desperate fingers. It was hard, painstaking work, but she kept at it with dogged determination, picking at the knot and trying to work it loose. She was close... Almost...there! Finally, she had it loose enough to slip out of her bindings. Her eyes sparkled to life. Taking a brief moment to make sure no one was coming, she quietly rushed to the attic window and opened it. The sound of a freight train filled the room, sailing by so quickly that it shook the house. Once the freight train had roared past, a stopped Amtrak was revealed on a side track, waiting for its turn to enter the small station.

* * *

The train still hadn't moved when Larry finally put out the joint and left the restroom, looking both ways to make sure no one saw him leaving the smoke-filled room with the distinctive odor of weed. Making his way back to the club car, he sat down and stared out the window, noticing a weathered stand-alone house surrounded by a broken wooden fence with chipped white paint. On the clothesline, droplets of water dripped from newly hung bedsheets as they whipped back and forth in the brisk breeze. Looking up to the second story window, he blinked twice and rubbed his bleary eyes before looking again. Amazingly, he spied an escaping female as she slid down the porch roof to the ground, taking a hard spill on the solid earth below.

Just then, a man ran out the front door of the house and began searching the yard, seeing nothing until the woman ran for the train. He took off after her, shouting, "come back here!"

When he caught up to her, they grappled with each other until a knife appeared out of nowhere. They both struggled for possession of the weapon. The fight continued until the woman kneed the man and jerked the blade from his hand, cutting him in the process. She paused only a moment before fleeing and vanishing from sight.

Larry looked everywhere for her, jumping out of his seat and running from window to window, but she was nowhere to be seen until…

Wham!

The sound startled him, and he jumped as the girl pounded her arms against the glass in front of him, her face streaked with blood. Her muffled cries came through the window. "Help me! Please, help me!"

Shocked, Larry fell backward against the seat across the aisle. Catching his breath, he stood up, but she was gone.

Frantically he shouted for help. "Conductor! Hey! Somebody needs help!"

Moving back to the window, he pressed his face to the glass to look down toward the track. At first, he didn't see anything, but then the woman jumped up again, her screams muffled by the hand of a dark figure. Then she was gone.

"Hey, stop!" Larry shouted, scanning the rail car for help.

"Somebody…anybody…we've got to help her!"

The few people in the car ignored him. Fear for the woman gave him a shot of adrenaline and drove some of his drunkenness from his brain. He raced through one car after the next until he found the one with the exit door. When he reached it, he tried to open the portal, but the security lock was in place, and he could not budge it. Panicked, he ran to the observation car, finding several passengers reading, eating, or working on their laptop computers in "library-like" silence.

"Did you see that girl?" Larry shouted, asking each person he passed.

The passengers briefly stopped what they were doing. They eyed him suspiciously before ignoring him and returning to what they were doing. Seeing Jamal and Quinn seated at the back of the car, reviewing her photo book, he raced to their seat.

"Did you see that girl trying to escape?"

They calmly shook their heads.

"No," Quinn replied.

"What, girl?" Jamal asked. "Someone here on the train?"

Larry grabbed them by the arm and pulled them to their feet, leading them down the aisle to a large, well-built conductor in the next car. The others piled up behind him, wondering what in the world was going on.

"I just saw a young woman escape from a house, and somebody grabbed her," Larry told the man.

Hesitantly, the conductor stopped checking the destinations over the seats of his newest passengers and turned to him. "Happens all the time around here. It probably was

49

someone's wife or sister sneaking out for the evening." He went back to checking destinations as the train lurched and started building speed.

"This is serious! There was a knife involved," Larry insisted, grabbing the man by the arm. "You can't tell me that a man would attack his wife or daughter with a knife unless…"

The conductor looked down at Larry's hand until it dropped. "Look, kid. I can't contact anybody out there to let them know that you think you saw something bad going on, and now that we're moving, I can't stop the train either. The tracks are too busy. We've got to maintain our time schedule, or we'll crash."

"Somebody's got to help that girl," Larry insisted. "We can't just stand here and do nothing!"

"I'm sorry. Train personnel can't get involved with someone who isn't a passenger. You want to help, get off the train." He examined his watch. "You've got ten minutes to decide before we reach the next station." He paused before continuing. "Although I wouldn't recommend it. Folks in these parts don't like strangers poking their noses into their business. Believe me. You'd be in more danger than that girl. These people are a different breed. Did you ever see the movie *Deliverance*?"

Jimmy, who just happened to be sitting in a seat close enough to hear the conversation, looked up and turned white. Larry grabbed Quinn's hand and pulled her back the way they had come, with Jamal following close behind. When they reached their seats, he stated in a firm voice, "We getting off the train."

"We are doing what?" Quinn asked. "Are you crazy? We can't do that. What about the wedding?"

"It's not every day I see a murder," Larry said, his voice filled with determination.

"What murder?" Jamal asked. "You didn't say anything about a murder, just that some girl needed help them."

"Well, I didn't exactly *see* a murder, but he did pull a knife. If you put two and two together…you get murder," Larry insisted.

"Huh? Are you sure you didn't dream this up?" Quinn asked. "You have had quite a bit to drink, you know?"

"I'm not experiencing some drunken delusion," Larry insisted. "I know what I saw."

"So you're saying that she could be dead by now?" Jamal asked.

"Dobson Valley coming up in five minutes," the Conductor said, poking his head through the door. No one else was getting off at this stop.

"What do you think, Jamal?" Quinn asked.

"We gotta do the right thing," he replied.

Chapter Six

The bar door whipped open with a crack as the Sheriff threw Bernadette's current boyfriend, Ted, against the large wooden shed behind the bar with a thud. Inside the shed, shadows filled the corners with streaks of light, forcing their way in between worn, unpainted boards. Shaky Pete was working in the darkened room when the thud against the wall froze his actions. He nervously looked out a peephole to see the Sheriff swing Ted around and shove him against the back wall of the bar. Pete fought to control his adrenaline surge as he pulled away from the secret hole. If the sheriff caught him there, he would be in a mess of trouble when Packy saw what was inside.

"Where were you last night?" Packy asked Ted.

"I was home," Ted stammered.

"Liar! You were out with Bernadette," the sheriff growled.

Ted screwed up his courage. "Just because yer stuck in the past doesn't mean the rest of us need to live in it, too. She's not yer woman any longer. You need to get that through your thick skull."

His words angered the Sheriff, and he pressed his forearm against Ted's throat. Packy was about to say more when he heard a noise that drew his attention to the wooden shed. Cocking his head slightly, he listened and waited.

Inside, Shaky Pete had tripped over something in the dark. He now pulled back to listen and wait. Fear of discovery made him sweat buckets until Packy shrugged and returned his attention to Ted.

"Katie is missing, and you were there at the house last night. That makes you a suspect to my way of thinkin'. What happened?"

"Nothing," Ted replied, his manner surly. "Bernadette and I went out for dinner and drinks, nothing more."

"Did you walk her to the front door?"

Bernadette had already told him the answer, but he wanted to confirm it with Ted.

"I don't know," Ted stammered. "No...I just dropped her off."

"Did you kiss her?"

"If I did, it's none of your business," Ted replied. "Is this about the missing girls or me dating a woman you couldn't commit to?"

The Sheriff shoved him away. "Don't let me catch you around that house again. I'm keepin' my eye on you."

Packy shoved him again and headed back into the bar.

* * *

Larry urgently pulled down their bags from the overhead rack while Quinn talked to the conductor about reissuing new tickets. Jamal scrambled to snatch up the group's carryon bags.

"It's like the conductor said. People are different out here," Jamal said, trying to reason with his friend. "They're not gonna like it if some city slickers suddenly show up in their town, talking about a kidnapping and accusing one of their fine citizens of murder, especially when one of the strangers is black."

"You're kidding, right?" Larry asked.

"This is a bad idea," Jamal insisted. "You know that, don't you?"

Larry turned to Quinn, who had just returned, and they both nodded. Then turning to Jamal, they stared at him until he finally gave in.

As the train pulled into the station, the rundown condition of the train depot matched that of the town. Rotted from age and neglect, it seemed like a forgotten time capsule. Larry and Quinn stumbled onto the wooden platform and eyed their surroundings. It was like arriving on some foreign planet. A toothless old man stood in front of a sliding glass window in the center of a tiny building, not much bigger than a small bedroom. Inside was a small desk, a two-drawer file cabinet, a small table that held an ancient percolator and coffee supplies, and a secretary's swivel chair. Two doors were visible through the window. One led outside. The other hid a small bathroom containing a sink and a toilet and little else. The old man watched while Jamal stood at the threshold with his luggage, still indecisive. Behind him, the conductor issued his final warning.

"I wouldn't get off here if I was you."

"Do I have a choice?" Jamal asked. His expression was bleak.

"What's the name of this town?" Quinn asked the conductor.

"Dobson Valley," he replied.

"Fine, fine, fine... Got your bags?" Larry impatiently asked.

Seeing that his warning had no effect, the conductor shook his head. "Next train arrives at nine in the morning. Try to keep yourselves in one piece till then."

Determined to contact the local law enforcement, Larry punched 911 into his cell phone, but when he held it to his ear, he heard nothing. He looked at the phone and realized that there was no signal.

"That's not going to work around here," the conductor said. "Mountains block the signal."

The conductor started to close the door, and a moment later, the train released its brakes.

"Dammit, Jamal, where's my camera?" A panicked Quinn asked as she checked the bags he was carrying.

Jamal shrugged. Jumping on-board, she rushed past the conductor like a mother trying to rescue her child from a burning building. The train nudged forward, with Larry and Jamal following her movements through the windows of the rail car.

"You've got to hurry, Miss," the conductor hollered.

"Stop the train!" Larry shouted.

"I can't," the conductor yelled. "Once it starts, there is no stopping."

They could barely see Quinn ransacking the overhead storage compartment. Quinn finally found her camera bag and raced back down the aisle against the train's motion. Seeing her, Larry ran alongside the doorway.

"Better hurry," the conductor shouted. "The train will soon be going too fast for you to safely debark, and I've got to get this door shut."

When she reached the door, Quinn jumped from the train car's steps right into Larry's arms. Disengaging herself, she shoved away from him as the conductor finally closed and locked the door. The three friends watched the train pick up speed and pulled away. They did not move until the last car's single red taillight trailed off into the darkening mountains. They were alone and on their own, facing an unknown town filled with backwards people who made them more than a little nervous and afraid. Quinn snapped a photo. As she did, long bony fingers reached out from behind her back and clutched her right shoulder. She screamed and spun around to see the toothless old bum sucking on his gums and grinning like a fool as he stood in front of them. He stared at the newcomers for several moments before speaking.

"Got any money?"

"Not now, old man," Larry said.

Jamal dug into his pocket for change, as did Quinn. They handed him a couple dollars.

"Peace, brother," Jamal said.

"What are you doing? Handing out liquor change? You know, that's what he'll use it for. Let's go," Larry grumbled.

"I ain't using it for drink," the bum said. His tone was a bit surly. "I just like asking fer money. Makes me feel good. Got no TV, too old for sex, and I've been kicked out of the bar. What else can I do?"

"Fine, fine," Larry said impatiently. "Let's go."

He grabbed his luggage, a new modern tote, while the others followed suit, pulling their heavy payloads along floorboards badly in need of refinishing. Jamal hefted an old blue suitcase from the '70s, while Quinn, who had clearly over packed, followed. Pulling two-wheeled cases that kept tipping over until the bum stepped in front of her, getting in her face.

"You ought not to be here, little girl. Things ain't what they seem. Pretty young things like you disappear around her. You could end up getting' yerself killed if you're not careful."

Quinn turned white and hurried to catch up with the guys. She glanced back to see if she was being followed, but the bum had disappeared.

With a shiver of dread, she inserted herself between Larry and Jamal and glanced around at their surroundings. The place looked like a ghost town in the making. Out-of-business signs hung on the doors of several empty storefronts and cracked windows told the story of the neglected buildings. The streets weren't much better. They were littered with potholes, and in some cases, the pavement had chipped away, leaving actual ruts in the road. One or two traffic lights hung darkly over the town's two intersections. They were broken and cracked with age.

"What a dump!" Jamal exclaimed.

As they walked down the street that was devoid of people, only two cars passed them. In the distance, a patron lit a cigarette and stepped into Shaky Pete's Bar. Even in the dim light of dusk, the three friends couldn't help noticing that many of the windows, doors, and telephone poles were plastered with what appeared to be hastily posted notices. Jamal spotted one on the ground and snatched it up. After a quick glance, he handed it to Larry. Quinn hurried over to see what the guys were looking at.

"That homeless man creeped me out," Quinn said. "He made it sound like I was going to get…"

"…killed?" Larry asked, looking up and finishing her sentence.

He showed her the paper in his hand, containing the pictures of twenty girls. Centered above the pictures was the word *MISSING*. Beneath the pictures, the words read.

NOTICE: If you have any information regarding the whereabouts of these girls, please contact Sheriff Packy or Deputy Dale. A $1000 reward is being offered for any information leading to the arrest and conviction of the person or persons responsible.

Quinn shivered. "Ah, what you say we make this quick, guys. The girl you saw trying to escape may be victim number twenty-one."

The sky turned darker, and the neon sign at Shaky Pete's flickered on, its color illuminating their faces with its garish light. As they approached the establishment, they heard the muffled sound of Lynyrd Skynyrd's song *Free Bird.* Jamal opened the door, and the music grew louder along with the sound of laughter, pool balls cracking against each other, and glasses clinking, followed by the noise of a bottle breaking.

The three stumbled inside with their luggage as their eyes adjusted to the neon beer signs and lights over the pool table. The scent of spilled beer and cigarette smoke was nearly overwhelming as it permeated the air. Looking around, the trio saw the heads and bodies of dead and stuffed animals covering the walls, making Quinn grimace in disgust and Jamal quiver. He hated the way humans needlessly killed animals. Displaying them as trophies disturbed him even more.

The customers were a mixed crowd, composed of mill workers, loggers, truck drivers, and construction workers. The patrons were playing pool, spitting tobacco, making selections at the jukebox, and spitting more tobacco. Nearly all were drinking beer. Shaky Pete tended bar. He watched the three strangers as they stepped up next to a seated bar hick, whose head wavered as he stared into his empty mug, wondering how it had gotten empty so quickly.

"Where's the Sheriff's office?" Larry asked.

"You're standing in it," the bar hick replied, his words mildly slurred.

Shaky Pete and the bar hick grinned as the rest of the customers laughed.

"Went home to sober up," Pete finally said. "Ya just missed him. He's here most days."

"And nights," the bar hick added, causing more laughter among the patrons.

"Could you call him? It's kinda important. "

Shaky Pete snapped his towel, killing a fly. "If he's asleep, believe me. He won't appreciate being woke up."

"This is an emergency!" Larry said a little too loudly. "We need to talk to him now!"

"And I'm telling you, he doesn't like to be disturbed," Pete warned.

"Look. I saw a woman escape through the attic window of a house while our train was sidetracked."

"Bart, your wife left again!" The bar hick shouted with a snort, causing more laughter.

"The man chasing her had a knife, and I believe he was going to hurt her," Larry insisted. "You've got to call him!"

At his distressed insistence, the patrons stopped laughing, and the noise level in the bar softened noticeably. Shrugging, Pete picked up the phone and dialed Packy's number.

Still fully dressed fully in his uniform, Sheriff Packy was face down on a battered old couch, his body contorted and lifeless except for an occasional window-rattling snore. The living room was disheveled and in dire need of being cleaned. Flies fought the breeze of an antique fan to feast on leftover chicken bones in a box of takeout that sat next to his service revolver. The phone rang, bringing a moan. With each ring, he twitched and moved a little more, finally picking up the receiver for no other reason than to stop what seemed like ear-shattering blasts that unmercifully clawed at his headache.

"What?" Packy growled, dazed, and irritated.

As Pete spoke, three pairs of eyes were fixed on him.

"Hey, Sheriff, it's Pete. I hate to bother ya, but we got worries here." The bartender kept his eyes on the three strangers. "You need to come over. Some Yankees from the train are rantin' and raving about a lady escapin' from a house where the trains get sidetracked. They said that the man chasing her was carryin' a knife in his hand."

His words brought the Sheriff to his feet and nearly sobered him up somewhat. This was the last thing he needed. His next thought brought him to full sobriety. What if the man they saw was the killer? But then his mind thought about where the train had to have been one. All this was happening.

"Dammit! You tell 'em to wait there. I'll be right over. Don't let them out of your sight." Hanging up the phone, he grabbed his sidearm and punched in a familiar number. "Hey! It's me," he said to the person on the other end of the line. "Do we have a problem?" He paused, listening to the response. "Where's she at, and what the hell happened?"

Back at the bar, Pete turned to the three strangers. "Sheriff's on his way. Didn't sound none too happy. He said you was to wait here for him." Giving them another grin, he pulled out a massive jar of pig's feet and a jar of pickled eggs from the shelf beneath the bar and plopped them down in front of them. "How about some pickled eggs…pig's feet…RC Cola…a Moon Pie? Name yer poison."

Repulsed, Larry and the others eyed the eggs and skinned animal feet eerily floating in the jars.

"Can a person get some moonshine around here?" Larry asked.

Pete gave him a stern look. "You may be from the big city, young fella, but you got to know that stuff ain't legal."

"Forget it," Larry replied in a bored voice. "I just wanted to try it. You do have a beer, right?"

Pete nodded. "Sure. We have Bud, Bud Light, Bud Draft, Bud Ice, Bud Ice Light, Big Bud, Little Bud, Bud Special, and Bud Classic."

The three-eyed each other. Apparently, Pete either didn't want to carry any other type of beer, or the other brewers wouldn't deliver to such an out-of-the-way place.

"Um, I guess I'll have a Bud," Larry replied.

"Me, too," Quinn added.

"Bud it is," Jamal said.

Pete kept his eyes fastened on Larry as he served the beers, while a couple of patrons admired Quinn's attractive figure.

Meanwhile, in an isolated wooden room, the woman Larry was so concerned about sitting on the edge of a small bed with a mattress that rested on wire springs. Holes of moonlight poked through the boarded-up windows. Frustrated, she jumped up and smashed an antique Bentwood chair against the boards until it shattered in her hands, and the door of the room slammed open, banging into the wall behind it. A shadowy figure in muddy boots appeared, filling the doorway.

"Be quiet and sit down! You misbehave again, and there'll be no supper for you."

The figure glowered at her. "You have certainly caused a fine mess of trouble. Now git down the basement and try to be a good little girl for me."

Knowing she had no other choice, the imprisoned female obeyed.

Chapter Seven

An oddly situated old car tire sat in the center of the bar floor. The yellow glow of the overhead light cascading over it like it was some kind of shrine. Looking to pass the time until the Sheriff arrived, Jamal touched it, wondering why it was there. His actions drew the attention of the crowd when, without thinking, he pulled back his leg to kick the tire.

"No!" Shaky Pete shouted. "I wouldn't do that if I were you."

But his cry was too late. Jamal's kick struck the tire, knocking it a couple of feet across the floor.

Thud!

The bar patrons flinched in unison. Then seemingly as one, they set their beers down and pushed back their chairs. Pool cues were dropped to the table, and the Lynyrd Skynyrd's record skipped to a halt as the crowd descended upon Jamal. As soon as he was aware of what was happening, his eyes grew as large as saucers, and he gulped as he backed away a few steps.

"No, wait a minute, fellas."

One man, in particular, a hairy specimen who could have been Sasquatch's distant relative, grabbed Jamal by the shirt and shoved him into the nearest wall. Butch spread his arms, holding back the others.

"Yer gonna die for that!" The hairy man growled.

"For kicking a tire?" Jamal asked incredulously. "For crying out loud, it's just a crummy old tire! The thing's even bald. Why would anyone want to keep it anyway?"

"That...*tire*...belonged to the King!" The bar hick said in a reverent voice.

"Elvis?" Jamal squeaked, wondering why anyone would want to keep an old tire as a souvenir. But then, he guessed that if it had belonged to Elvis, he could possibly see why they would want to keep it.

The crowd moved aggressively closer.

"No, *the King*," the bar hick snarled. "Richard Petty, the king of NASCAR, and the greatest driver that ever lived."

Larry elbowed his way to the front of the crowd. "That's right. The *King*! Two hundred victories, seven-time winner of the Winston Cup, ten consecutive wins in 1967 – a record that still stands, and a member of Motorsports Hall of Fame. Richard Petty is the *King*. This is his *tire*!" Larry ended with a shout, and he punched the air with his fist.

The crowd took off their hats, and a quiet moment of reverence filled the room as another patron moved the tire back in place and stepped back as the crowd bowed to the tire.

"But the King is *not* a good man," Larry said.

The crowd broke their focused meditation and turned their hostile gazes on him. Jamal stared at him in shock.

"Are you nuts?" He whispered out of the side of his mouth. "These guys are going to kill us."

"No, my friends. The King is a *great* man. And the King would never hold it against this ignorant fool for not knowing. It wouldn't be right. Let us be like the King and let this *idiot* go."

The crowd visibly softened as they masticated his words in their minds.

"He's right," Butch said at last. "Let the idiot go."

As everyone returned to what they were doing before Jamal had kicked the tire, the bar hick, who went by Butch, Wilson, Hank, and Leonard sauntered over to Quinn. Wilson, a former miner and vetran of the bar, obviously had no perception of personal space, and when he stepped in front of her, his mouth was mere inches from her face. Quinn stepped back in disgust, wrinkling her nose and squinting her watering eyes in reaction to his bad breath.

Wilson turned and looked at Jamal. "Are you her boyfriend?"

"No," Jamal answered, backing up a step. The last thing he wanted to do was get into another altercation with these crazy people.

"What about you?" The obnoxious bar fly asked Larry.

"Yes," Larry replied.

"No," Quinn answered at the same time. "He's not my boyfriend."

"Okay, boys," Wilson hooted. "We got us a single lady. Let's *dance*!"

The jukebox instantly began to howl a lively mountain tune. The patrons cheered as Wilson reached over and grabbed Quinn's butt to escort her to the dance floor. Enraged, she spun around and cracked her bottle of beer over his head, spilling most of its contents on him and the floor.

The room seemed to freeze, filling it with a hushed, ominous silence. Then as if on cue, a massive bar brawl ensued. Chairs, bottles, and glasses of beer flew through the air, making the room a circus of confusion. A stray bottle soared upward, hitting the deer head on the nearby wall. It fell, striking Butch on the top of his head and shattered. Then as quickly as the fight had begun, the room froze once more, becoming abruptly motionless as Sheriff Packy came through the door and walked across the room toward the bar.

"Enough!" He shouted. "What in Sam Hill is going on here?"

No one said a word until the silence was broken by a bottle crashing to the floor behind the Sheriff's back. Packy narrowed his eyes and scanned the crowd, daring anyone to make a move.

"Hank, what the hell are you doing gettin' into a fight? I thought you were smarter than that."

Bald, mousy Hank had the good sense to look sheepish. He stared down at the floor a moment before looking up and replying in a squeaky voice. "But, Sheriff, that Yankee girl was beatin' us up."

Packy looked at him in disbelief before turning to the man beside him. "Luke, if your wife ever found out you were fightin' in the bar, you would be banned from here for life." He pinned another man with his gaze. "And Leonard, you're a Deacon for crying out loud! This ain't no way to treat guests! These are fine people who cared enough about the fate of some poor woman to delay their trip, get off the train, and report the trouble. They're trying to be neighborly. You should be ashamed of yourself. Apologize right now."

"Yes, sir," Leonard said. Turning to Quinn and the others, he blushed and said, "Regrets." Then he hung his head and return to his seat at one of the tables.

The other bar patrons also murmured an apology. "Sorry."

"Now, I want everybody to git down and help Pete clean up this mess," Packy said, looking at the trio he had verbally chastised. Then turning to the strangers, he said, "Get yer bags. Yer comin' with me."

Then he marched toward the door, which Jamal quickly jumped in front of and held open. The Sheriff gave him an odd look, shook his head, and walked past him. Outside in the deserted street, Sheriff Packy lit a cigarette, his back toward the group. As he pocketed his lighter, he turned sharply and faced the three friends.

"All right, what the hell is this about?" He asked curtly. "So some young girl ran from a house with a knife. Who gives a fat rat's ass?"

His words froze the trio in their tracks, throwing them off guard. Larry straightened and moved closer to the sheriff.

"She was being chased by someone."

"You saw this from the train? Did the engineer, conductor, or any other passengers see this?"

"I don't think so," Larry admitted.

"What about you two?" Packy asked Jamal and Quinn.

They shook their heads no but otherwise remained silent.

"Did you get a visual on the two people involved in this here incident?" Packy asked Larry.

"Yes...well, sort of, given the circumstances. It happened so fast, but I remember the exact spot where it happened."

The Sheriff scowled. "You got off the train and woke me up for that? This sort of thing happens all the time. It's nothing more than some farmer's teenage daughter, trying to slip one past her old man and have a night of fun. I ought to throw your stupid Yankee ass in jail right now for all the trouble you're causing. Instead, I'm gonna give you one chance to walk your city-slicker self back to the depot and get the hell out of town on the next train."

Quinn grabbed her friend's arm. "Come on, Larry, let's go."

Happy to be shut of this crazy town, Jamal grabbed his bags and started walking toward the train depot. He only moved a couple steps when Larry spoke, making him close his eyes and bow his head. He thought *This is it. We're dead, or at least, we'll probably end up in a jail cell for the rest of the night.*

"No way," Larry said to Quinn. "Just because I'm the only one who witnessed it, doesn't mean it didn't happen. This is stupid. One of them had a knife for crying out loud, which they fought over! You can't tell me that a father and daughter would be fighting over a knife." Larry stepped forward, getting in the Sheriff's face. "Listen up, small-town Sheriff, I know what I saw! She ran up to my window, covered in blood. Someone grabbed her, and she fought back while being dragged away. Someone's life is in danger, and I won't be forced onto a train without making sure she gets rescued!"

Sheriff Packy angrily grabbed Larry by the arm and performed a well-trained maneuver, twisting his arm and jerking it up behind his back, pinning Larry face down to the hood of the Jeep. "Don't you push me, son. Don't even think about it. You'd better be 100 percent correct about this, or I'll have your balls so tight in a sling, you'll be crooning, *Fly Me to the Moon* in a high soprano. Now say, 'I understand.' "

Larry's muffled voice came from the hood of the Jeep. "I understand."

"Your friends can't hear you, scumbag. Louder!"

"I understand!" Larry shouted.

The Sheriff shoved him to the ground. "Put your bags in the back of the Jeep. We'll go take a look at that area you saw this happen and get this straightened out once and for all. Then I'll give you a ride back to the depot. Just so you don't go wandering off and causing more trouble."

* * *

Tears made Katie's mascara run down her cheeks, and her hair was matted and dirty. A motion-sensitive toy clown stood in a corner across from where she sat, releasing a hauntingly evil laugh every time she moved. She awkwardly reached around behind her chair for the bowl of food left there. Her fingers sank into something mushy, and as she brought it around in front of her. It looked and felt like maggots were crawling on her skin. Katie shrieked and threw the bowl into the corner. It landed in a beam of moonlight, coming through the boarded-up window, and she saw that it was only rice. Her stomach growled, and she cried, wishing she had not thrown the food to the floor in a moment of panic. She had no idea if or when she would be fed again.

* * *

Deputy Dale stepped out of the shadows, humming a happy show tune. His unbuttoned uniform shirt revealed a wife-beater undershirt as he carried a tray containing chicken and rice soup, a small stack of crackers, a glass of milk, and a pitiful looking daisy into an old wooden room.

"Eat up. I need you healthy," he told the shadow of a lady, sitting in the corner of the room. "I have to go to work now, but don't you worry none. I'll return home soon enough. And I promise, will spend lots of time together."

69

He placed the food on a small round table next to the chair and left, whistling the same tune.

* * *

The Sheriff's Jeep darted down a rutted dirt road. He knew he was driving too fast, but he wanted to get this unwelcome task over with as soon as possible. These Yankees would never understand the situation. And he had no intention of letting them in on the town secret. His passengers' hands tightly gripped the door handles as they tried to pin down the direction they needed to go. Exchanging uncomfortable glances, Jamal and Quinn silently cursed Larry as they worried. To their way of thinking, the Sheriff did not seem to care about the murders going on in this town. And they couldn't help wondering if the girl Larry had seen from his train window would be the next poster to occupy space on the telephone poles. Empty cigarette packages, fast food wrappers, and brown stained paper cups rolled around the floor as Packy drove.

"Where did it happen?" He asked.

"I think it was an old white farmhouse with a worn picket fence badly in need of a paint job," Larry replied.

Packy snorted. "That describes just about every house in the valley."

"There was laundry hanging out on a clothesline," Larry offered.

"Not helping. Folks around here can't afford clothes dryers. Everyone hangs their laundry on a line outside to dry."

Exasperated, Larry added, "I'm guessing it was about a mile before the depot."

Still, traveling entirely too fast for the bad road, the Jeep skidded sideways. The Sheriff didn't seem to notice. He hoped that at his current speed, Larry would be unable to recognize the spot he was looking for. Still, he had to make it look like he was actually trying to find a spot.

"Could be over by Mule Crossing," Packy said thoughtfully. "That's one place trains get sidetracked."

The Sheriff made an abrupt turn into a batch of trees, causing his three passengers to brace for a collision. Somehow, the Jeep missed the trees and landed on an unnoticeable path of packed earth. The vehicle broke through a small creek to an open field, revealing the Shelby Farm, barely visible in shadows. The house seemed to fit the description Larry had given. Packy killed the engine, and the unfamiliar sounds of the woods surrounded them. Larry strained to see in the dark.

"What do ya think?" The Sheriff asked.

"I don't know…" Larry said. "It's kinda hard to see from here."

"Get out and take a closer look," Packy told him.

Grass, wet from earlier rain, brushed against Larry's pant legs as he stepped out of the vehicle and walked into the surrounding darkness. As he did, he noticed shadows moving through the bushes. Was someone hiding there, or was it simply his overactive imagination?

Quinn and Jamal peered out through the windows, straining to see.

"I don't see a house out there," Quinn said.

"Where's the Sheriff?" Jamal asked, wondering where he had gone.

Outside, failing to notice that he seemed to be alone, Larry continued talking. "It looks the same except…"

Suddenly, there was a flash, followed by a blast of gunfire.

Bang!

A branch was blasted into pieces only inches from Larry's head. Another blast quickly followed, and bark exploded from the same tree. Frightened for his life, he broke into a run. Footsteps and heavy breathing followed closely behind, causing him to put on a burst of speed.

"Run!" Jamal shouted to Larry through the open window of the passenger door.

Quinn reached over and turned on the police headlights and emergency lights. As Larry headed toward the vehicle, a huge German shepherd lunged toward him. Its jaws opened to take a bite out of his leg. Eighty-five pounds of solid dog crashed into him, knocking Larry into the door next to Quinn. She screamed, fearing for her friend's life. A moment later, the dog dropped on top of Larry and rolled over limp. Looking up from his position on the ground, he saw the Sheriff standing there with a stun gun. Larry pushed the dog away and scrambled up.

"Is that the house?" Packy asked nonchalantly.

"That dog almost killed me!" Larry shouted. *Did he bring me here on purpose, knowing this would happen?* He asked himself. "And why were you shooting at me."

"I wasn't the one shooting at you. Now is that the house?" Packy asked again.

Larry was too agitated to answer the question. "Then there's a redneck with a shotgun shooting at us! Are all you people insane around here?"

Then porch lights turned on, revealing Shelby standing twenty feet away, holding a shotgun and surrounded by the rest of his dogs.

"Sorry, Sheriff, just keepin' a lookout for trouble. What with all these girls disappearin', a man can't be too careful when it comes to keepin' his daughter safe."

The Sheriff waved. "It's okay, Shelby. No one was hurt."

Larry studied the farmhouse. "The porch didn't have a rail," he said thoughtfully. "And there wasn't a woodpile on the side either. This isn't the right house."

Packy scratched his head. "I don't know what to tell ya. This house is all there is out here."

"Damn, I really hate dogs," Larry said, warily eyeing the pack surrounding the farmer. Turning to Quinn, he said, "Let's get the hell out of here and get back to the train station where it's safe! The sooner we board Amtrak, the quicker we'll arrive at our destination."

* * *

Inside the wooden room, the female, who had tried to escape earlier, heard muffled gunshots in the distance. She winced and wondered if someone had been shot.

* * *

Larry and the Sheriff climbed back into the Jeep and turned it around. A long trail of ghostly dust followed the vehicle's red tail lights as it sped back down the dirt road. Looking out his window, Larry still searched for the house, positive that it had to be around here somewhere.

"Stop!" He suddenly shouted as another house that fit the description came into view.

Sheriff Packy slammed on brakes, and dust surrounded the car. As it slowly cleared, another white house with a picket fence was revealed.

"That's it," Larry said excitedly. "I'm pretty sure." He looked around. "Isn't that the railroad tracks up there?"

Packy swallowed the alarm that had risen inside. He had hoped that when he drove past this place, Larry wouldn't notice it. "That house? That's not it. It can't be."

"No. I'm pretty sure it is," Larry insisted.

The Sheriff put the Jeep into gear, apparently dismissing Larry's suggestion. "No, you're wrong."

"Wait, wait, wait!" Larry cried. "There's the woodpile."

"Where?" Packy asked, purposely looking everywhere but the spot where he knew the wood was stacked.

"There!" Larry said. "That's it! I'm positive. It's all there. Everything I saw."

Packy pulled to a stop, and Larry jumped out of the Jeep, Jamal and Quinn quickly following, but the Sheriff still hesitated.

"You're crazy," Packy said, sighing in resignation and getting out at last.

"Why?" Quinn asked. "What's wrong?"

"That's Mayor Farlow's house. That's what's wrong. Ain't no way the Mayor is involved in any wrongdoing."

Chapter Eight

Larry was stunned, and for a second, he wondered if he had gotten the wrong house. He looked to see if any of the houses close by had a tree similar to the one in the back of the house he had seen from the train. None did.

"Mayor's house or not, that's the one she came from."

Packy scowled. "Mayor's not going to like being disturbed because of your foolishness at this time of night."

"Just because he's the Mayor, doesn't mean he can't also be a kidnapper and a murderer," Larry snapped. "And if he is this evil person that has been killing the town's young women, who cares if he likes it or not? Don't you want to stop him before he kills someone else?"

"You just hold your mouth, boy," the Sheriff said. "Don't need some half-baked city boy flingin' accusations at the Mayor. I'll handle this."

The four of them piled out of the Jeep and approached the front door. Packy whipped his hat off his head and held it. Then raising his right hand, he rapped firmly on the door.

"He also happens to be the head of the school board and the volunteer Fire Chief," he said as they waited for the Mayor. "Ain't nobody more concerned about the townsfolk than he is."

He pounded on the door for several minutes before it finally opened. Standing on the front stoop, Sheriff Packy, Larry, Jamal, and Quinn blinked when the porch light switched on, and the door opened, revealing the Mayor in a brown silk robe with a brandy snifter in one hand and a fine cigar in the other.

"Sheriff Packy?" Mayor Farlow asked, surprised. "Lordy, what are you doing here? I hired a deputy so that you could take the night off and rest. If you're gonna work nights anyway, I may as well save the town some money and get rid of the deputy."

When he finished speaking, he noticed the three strangers crowded around the Sheriff.

"Apologies, Mayor Farlow. Sorry to bother you this time of night," Packy said.

"Who are these young folk? This is a little awkward, Sheriff. What's this about?"

"Official business, I'm afraid. These 'out-of-towners' here had Pete call and wake me up, saying they had seen a woman escaping from your house. I tried to tell him they were crazy, but they insisted on checking it out."

The Mayor laughed, and Sheriff Packy soon joined in with a chuckle.

"My lands, I'd never heard of such a thing…a woman? Well, I hate to admit this, but I haven't had a woman in this house for years! But you are right about one thing... If she did escape, I'd surely chase her!" He laughed again.

"You mind telling me where you were and what you were doing about, oh, say an hour ago?" Packy asked.

"Well, let's see," the Mayor said. It was obvious that he thought of this as nothing more than some kind of joke. "I made supper, and then I went upstairs to relax and enjoy a little reading…thus my wardrobe."

The Sheriff turned and eyed the three friends, his look clearly dismissing them and their suspicions. "Well, I think that's about all for now. Sorry to trouble you, Mayor."

"Now, wait just one minute!" Larry demanded. "What makes you so sure he doesn't have someone in there right now? He could be hiding her. Do you always take what a person says at face value?"

Quinn and Jamal stood with Larry, nervously nodding in agreement.

"Now hold on there, son. That's a mighty powerful accusation. I'm a well-respected member of this community. This is just a bunch of foolishness. I've got nothing to hide."

"Then I guess you won't mind if we have a look inside, will you?" Larry asked.

Packy narrowed his eyes, his expression stern. "Now you listen here. Let me handle this. I'm the Sheriff. Besides being our esteemed Mayor and Fire Chief, he is also the judge." He turned back to the Mayor. "It seems we got some mighty stubborn firecrackers here. I'm afraid I'm gonna officially have to ask if I can come in and take a look around yer house."

"And if I refuse?" The Mayor asked, his expression unreadable.

"Then you'll just have to issue me a search warrant." The Sheriff winked at the Mayor, but the three friends barely noticed.

"Fine, fine, I've no problem letting you get your eye full. No warrant needed."

"This really isn't necessary, Patrick."

"No, no, come on in. I insist. Can I get you youngins some lemonade?"

The Mayor gave the Sheriff a nodding signal.

As they trooped inside the living room, they spotted various pictures on the wall, revealing generations of local history. An old-time radio stood in the center of one wall, playing static ladened mountain music, and an antique table fan clicked in the corner next to a well-used recliner. Both sounds barely covered a scratching noise coming through the ceiling.

"Mind your manners," Packy said as he began a cursory search of the downstairs rooms.

While he was in the kitchen, Larry quietly started up the staircase.

"Hey! Hold it right there," Packy shouted as he returned to the living room and saw him halfway up the steps. "I'll not have you snooping around on your own. I'm the Sheriff, and I'll do the searching around here."

"If you think it will make things more peaceful, Packy, maybe you should take the young man upstairs with you. I would hate for this to keep lingering in their minds. Nothing like loose thoughts to stir up trouble, if you know what I mean."

He winked at the Sheriff, and this time, Quinn saw it.

Packy and Larry moved slowly up the steps. When they reached the top landing, noises emitted from behind a closed wooden door, firing up Larry's suspicions since all the other doors stood open. The Sheriff removed his baton as he listened closely at the door before swinging it open. A bat flew at their heads, startling both men. Inside, they saw only empty boxes stacked around the room.

Downstairs, the Mayor opened the front door and chased the bat out with a broom. Then closing the door, he retrieved a tray with glasses and served the last of a pitcher of lemonade. Quinn looked around, eyeing another group of photos with interest. As she did, she caught a glimpse of a woman's red shoe sticking out from beneath a cabinet. She quickly brought up her camera and shot a picture.

"Hey!" The Mayor called startled. "None of that. I don't like strangers taking pictures of my home." He covertly kicked the shoe into hiding under the cabinet. "Can I get you something else while you're waiting?"

Seeing the Sheriff and Larry coming down the stairs, Quinn and Jamal shook their heads no.

"Thanks a lot," Packy said. "Sorry again for troubling you."

"Not at all," the Mayor said. "Glad to help, what with everything going on around here, your work is appreciated."

Jamal and Quinn drained their glasses and returned them to the tray before turning and leaving. As the Mayor closed the door, Packy scrutinized Larry with a look of disbelief.

"I know what I saw," Larry insisted.

The four of them piled into the Jeep, and Packy drove them back to the train station. Getting out, he dropped their bags to the ground and turned to leave.

"That's it? No arrests? No further investigation?" Larry asked sarcastically. "Why am I not surprised?"

The Sheriff returned to his vehicle and put the Jeep in gear. Leaning out the window, he said, "Don't leave this place, or I will make an arrest! Damn, I hate nosy, good for nothing Yankees," he said as he drove off.

* * *

Katie lay on her side, struggling against the ropes that bound her hands and feet. Fresh and dried blood mingled on her wrists and arms from where the ropes had cut into her skin. Concentrating, she flopped around on the floor, eyeing the clown as she wiggled closer to it. With her bonded limbs, she awkwardly smashed its porcelain body. Its laugh eerily melted away. She was about to grab a piece to saw through her ropes when she heard footsteps and froze. Suddenly an eye watched her through a peephole. It just watched...

"Please! Please, let me out. Let me go home...please!" Katie cried, her voice still muffled by the gag in her mouth. "I know you're watching me. Let me out!"

* * *

In the alley behind his bar, Shaky Pete slipped out of an old wooden shed. He checked the area, making sure that it was clear. He was about to move away when he heard the sound of breathing coming through the door.

"Damn it!"

He slipped back inside, and the sound stopped. Checking the peephole one last time, he hurriedly sneaked out and locked the door, peeking through the hole one last time before returning to the bar.

Packy returned to the Sheriff's station, still disgruntled with the three Yankees. The office was simple, containing a table, four chairs, two desks, and a holding cell. Walking across the room, he poured himself a sober-up cup of coffee, which he sipped as he sat behind his desk. He propped his feet on it and analyzed the missing girl photos on the wall. On a large map, he followed each girl to the location where her body had been dumped.

"Yer a loser," a drunken man from the holding cell in the back said. Years of heavy drinking had reddened his nose and prematurely aged the man. "This has been going on for two years now, and you can't even find a small town killer. Mark my words,

Sheriff. He ain't through yet. Yer a lousy detective. This is why ya couldn't make it in the big city. Some FBI agent you turned out to be. No wonder they kicked you out. Why you couldn't even help yer own wife and kid. Never did find the one that caused their death, did ya?"

A series of memories flew through Packy's mind like an old-time black and white movie.

* * *

He was on night patrol, cruising around the town in his Jeep. At the local grade school, his daughter was in the school play. Her part called for her to be dressed up like a doll. In the audience, her mother watched the play, smiling and clapping, an empty seat beside her where the sheriff should have been.

The night slowly passed, and as the audience left to go home, Packy pulled over a young man speeding through town. He was writing the man a ticket when his radio went off. There had been a terrible accident. When he arrived on scene, he saw a familiar white late-model SUV wrapped around a tree, the victim of a drunk, hit and run driver. Inside the SUV, his wife and daughter were entangled in the wreckage, bloody and dying.

Packy called for more help and hurried over to the vehicle. He couldn't reach his wife. Her side of the car was smashed into the tree trunk. Running to the other side, he wrenched open the passenger side door and pulled his daughter from the wreckage. As he did, he checked his wife's pulse and discovered that she was already dead. Returning to his daughter, he rocked her as he waited for help, but the ambulance arrived too late, and she died in his arms, blood from a nasty head wound streaking her stage makeup.

Packy returned to reality with a jerk and a sob. He angrily threw his coffee cup against the wall, smashing it.

"Damn it! It's a lie," he said as he absentmindedly watched the coffee run down the wall. "I was a good agent. I just couldn't handle the pressure."

"Ha! Didn't get away from the pressure here, did ya? Thought you'd have an easy time of it here, did just? Well, he's still out there, Sheriff! And you ain't any closer to catching him now than you were when he made his first kill, and you know it."

Filled with rage, Packy marched to the jail cell, where the drunk stood, pressing his face against the bars. He grabbed the man by the collar and pulled back his fist.

"Go ahead, hit me. That's right. Hit me! He's beating you! So you beat me," the drunk slurred. "Ain't gonna do you no good, anyway."

Disgusted, the Sheriff shoved him to the floor of the cell.

"I ain't saying anything you don't know, except for one thing..." the drunk continued.

"Go to sleep," Packy said with a sigh as he headed back to his desk chair.

"I see things better behind bars than you do up close. Look again."

"At what?" Packy shouted in frustration.

"The pictures," the drunk said.

Packy studied the pictures. "What am I supposed to see? What is it?"

"Let me outta here." It was as though the drunk had forgotten what he was talking about earlier. "I'm not going to hurt anybody. I'll go straight home. And I won't tell anybody what I know."

Packy unlocked the door. "Tell me, damn it. What is it you see that I don't?"

"It's *you*! Ha! Don't you see? Yer the connection to all them missing girls!"

The drunk's words shook him, but he refused to believe them.

"Yer scum," Packy said as he shoved the drunk out the back door. Eying the photos across the room, he saw in his mind his little girl dressed up with doll-like make-up, hair, and dress. She was supposed to look like Raggedy Ann. Staring at the pictures for several moments, he finally realized that all of the victims were dressed just like his dead daughter had been on that terrible night. What if the drunk was right? But how could he be? His daughter hadn't been murdered. She had died in a car crash. Shaking his head in disgust, he marched to his desk, opened one of the drawers, and removing a bottle of whiskey, he took a hefty swallow.

* * *

As soon as the eye went away, Katie pulled at her bonds with her teeth, clawing at them with desperate fingers while she worked through the pain. Frustrated, she retrieved a piece of the broken porcelain clown head and began to saw at the ropes. It took several moments, but eventually, she was able to cut through the ropes. As one hand broke free, her exhausted expression came to life. Suddenly, Katie heard footsteps on the stairs. She briefly stopped and then quickly slipped the rope off her ankles.

She jumped to her feet and dashed to the boarded-up window with its cracks filled with moonlight. First, she tried to pull on the boards, hoping to work them loose, but they wouldn't budge. So she decided to climb up some of the stacked boxes to reach the ones higher up. Grabbing the top board, she realized that it was loose and began wiggling it. It was about to pop loose when she heard footsteps approaching. The footsteps grew closer,

83

and Katie hid in a dark corner, just as the door opened. The captor looked around the darkened room and seeing that the window was still boarded up, finally closed the door. Katie waited until the footsteps faded to make her move. Returning to the window, she pulled out the top board, revealing a toy doll hanging by a rope that had been knotted around its neck. The sight deeply shocked her, and she wondered if that would be her fate if she didn't escape.

Fear gave her a surge of adrenaline, and she frantically began working at the rest of the boards. After removing the last one, she fumbled with the locks and tugged the window up, but it only opened a few inches. The sound of a distant freight train filled the room, covering the noise she made, and she pushed harder until the window was halfway open. Then she crawled out onto the porch roof. She was nearly out with only her legs from the knees down, still remaining in the room. But before she could go any further, her legs were suddenly grabbed by the dark intruder, and she was pulled back inside and thrown to the floor with a snarl.

"I'll stay," Katie begged. "I swear. I'll stay. *Really*! I promise. I won't leave. And I won't cry. I know you don't like it when I cry. See...I'm not crying. Just don't kill me. Please. I'll do whatever you want."

Her captor didn't say a word but stared at her with cold, unfeeling eyes – eyes that seemed as dead as those of the doll hanging in the window.

* * *

a large, hairy, man crept down the street in a pickup truck and sneered at the three figures standing at the train station. His truck backfired, sounding like several gunshots, and they caused Larry, Quinn, and Jamal to hit the ground. The hairy man laughed and peeled away. A moment later, they picked themselves up and dusted themselves off.

"Hey, I'm sorry about all of this," Larry apologized. "I really thought that all we had to do was tell the Sheriff what I saw, and he would handle it. How was I to know that the law here doesn't really seem to care?"

"Don't worry about it," Jamal said.

When she didn't say anything, Larry walked over to Quinn. "You okay?"

"I was scared, Larry," she said, her voice quavering a bit. "I thought… I thought." She left the sentence unfinished.

"So did I," Larry admitted. "You don't have to worry about that now. We're getting out of here."

"We can't," Quinn said, surprising him.

"What?"

She powered up her camera. "You were right. I saw something at the house…a woman's red shoe. The Mayor tried to hide it, but not before I managed to snap a picture of it."

She revealed the photo on the camera. Jamal stepped up to her other side so that he, too, could see the picture.

"Hey, it's a woman's shoe," Jamal said. "So what?"

"Maybe he likes prancing about in women's clothing?" Larry suggested.

Quinn shook her head. "That shoe was too small for him. Where was the other one? Besides, did you see how big his feet were? And it looked brand new, too. He said that a woman hadn't been in his home for years. If that was true, why would he have a woman's shoe in his home?"

"Why didn't you say something to the Sheriff?" Larry asked. "Instead, you left me hanging out to dry."

"I don't believe the Sheriff would have done anything. He wants us to leave town. I don't know why, but I caught the Mayor winking at him like there was some kind of secret between them."

"Now that I think of it," Jamal said, "I did hear a noise of some kind upstairs."

"What do you mean?" Larry asked. "Are you saying they're both kidnappers?"

"No," Quinn replied, drawing out the word. "I don't know, but I do know what I saw. Something is fishy here."

"And I know what I heard," Jamal added. "It sounded like someone was upstairs. And unless he had a lover up there that he wanted to keep secret, something was making that noise."

"It was just a bad that had gotten in," Larry said.

"Maybe so, but the sounds I heard sure didn't sound like a bat," Jamal insisted.

Making up his mind, Larry dragged their luggage into a utility closet and shoved it inside. "We're going back."

"There might be another problem," Quinn said thoughtfully.

"What?" Larry asked.

"Did you see the photos on the wall?"

Both guys shook their heads.

"I think the Sheriff and the Mayor are brothers," Quinn said, stunning them with her revelation.

"But that can't be. They have different last names," Larry protested.

"So what? They could have the same mother but different fathers. Divorce is so common these days. She may have had one baby, got divorced, remarried, and then had the other. Wouldn't be a bit surprising," Quinn said wisely.

"Which makes them even more suspicious," Larry said. "It sure seems like they're working in cahoots. Come on. We're going back."

The three friends jogged down the tracks. It was the quickest way to return to the so-called scene of the crime, especially since they were uncertain of how else to get there. They had been too upset to really notice what roads the Sheriff was taking. A moment later, Quinn screamed.

"Jamal, Larry, watch out!"

A flash of white light bore down upon them, and the ground shook with the thunderous sound of a roaring freight train headed straight for them. Its horn blasted a warning, and they jumped into the ditch, Quinn on one side, the guys on the other. When the train was finally past, she climbed back on the tracks but did not see her friends.

"Jamal! Larry!"

When they did not respond, she became frantic and ran down the tracks, looking for their dead bodies. But she found no sign of them. Unwilling to give up, Quinn wandered through the trees for some time until she heard a moan.

"Larry? Jamal?" Quinn called. "Are you there?"

"Shhh," Jamal whispered.

Quinn searched the area finding nothing. Then the moan became a scream.

"Up here," Jamal called softly. Looking up, she spotted him and Larry in the tree branches above her head.

"You're alive! How'd you get up there?" She asked, puzzled. "I've been worried sick."

This time both Larry and Jamal shushed her, but their eyes were fixed on a distant farmhouse. Another scream sounded, and as she looked around until she spotted a window that they were eagerly watching. As she focused on it, she saw a silhouette of a perfectly shaped naked woman having sex.

"Hey," someone muttered. "Mind sliding over a bit? You're in my way."

Quinn searched the tree until she found the same toothless bum they had first met when getting to this place. But this time, he was sitting on a branch, smoking a corncob pipe.

"What are you doing?" Larry asked, surprised that he hadn't noticed the bum before.

"Same as you," the bum chuckled. "Enjoying the best moaner west of the Yadkin River. It's Saturday night. With Krissy's husband out of town, this love affair is the best show around!"

Quinn looked disgusted. "Obviously, that woman has no shame. Who in the world would want to do it in a window unless they were an exhibitionist? Come on, we're here to save a woman, and this one clearly doesn't need saving, except maybe spiritually."

Quinn yanked the two guys down to the ground, and they fell on their backs with a loud thud. Almost immediately, the moaning stopped, and lights came on. The male lover ran out outside naked as a jaybird, holding a shotgun. Everyone ran for their lives as shots were fired at their retreating backs.

* * *

Mayor Patrick Farlow drank a cool, freshly made glass of lemonade and replaced his silk robe with a bloodied apron. Hefting a butcher knife, he uncovered what appeared to be a bloodied corpse in the sink. Whistling a tune, he skillfully chopped away, separating the parts into manageable pieces.

Chapter Nine

Humming along with the Barry Manilow song *Mandy*, Deputy Dale patrolled Dobson Valley and its outskirts. When he turned onto Lover's Lane, he spotted a '79 Ford Pinto parked on a clearing overlooking the town. Curious, he pulled up behind the vehicle and retrieved his flashlight from the glove compartment, shined it toward the back window of the car. At first, he didn't see anyone inside, but a moment later, he caught a glimpse of a young woman and man struggling in the front seat. Jumping out, Dale drew his gun and threw caution to the wind, hurried up to the driver's side of the vehicle and pounded on the door. "Hold up. Okay, with going on in there?" he asked, pointing his service revolver through the open window at the man's head.

The startled couple turned frightened eyes on him. Getting caught would be a tremendous problem if the deputy decided to contact their fathers and tell on them.

"Darlene? Darlene Tucker?" The Deputy said, straining to see inside. "Tommy Wallace, is that you? What are you two kids up to? "

Shining the light into the vehicle, he saw that it was indeed Darlene and Tommy, their hair messed up, and their clothes partially unbuttoned. They had obviously been making out pretty heavily.

"Yes, sir," Darlene replied, embarrassed. She quickly pulled her blouse back over her bra and began buttoning it up as fast as her fingers could fly.

Deputy Dale grinned at the sight and holstered his weapon. "Does your momma know you're out so late with Tommy here? I'll bet she doesn't."

"We weren't doing anything wrong," Tommy said, his tone defensive. "We love each other and want to get married."

"I'm not talking to you, boy," Dale growled, his expression turning to a scowl. "You'd best get on home, and don't you let me catch you fondling Sam Tucker's daughter again. Ya hear? You know what that old man would do to ya if he ever found out? You're a fool boy. You get her pregnant, and you won't have to worry about a shotgun weddin'…just the shotgun."

"Yes, sir," Tommy mumbled. "Sorry. You ain't gonna tell anybody, are you? We really do wanna get hitched."

"Get on home," Dale said. But as Tommy tried to start the car, the Deputy laid a hand on his shoulder and shook his head. "Not you, Darlene. Come on, girl. Get in my car. The streets around here aren't safe these days."

"I'll be okay with Tommy. I promise it'll take me right home," Darlene said.

"It's late. If you show up at the door with Tommy, your dad is going to know what was going on. It's best if I take you home," the deputy said.

"But it'll be even worse if they see you bringing me home," Darlene said, fretting. "He'll wanna know what was going on for sure."

"Just you listen here to me, Darlene. I can always make up some story, but I'm telling ya. It's for the best that you don't go home with Tommy."

Darlene hesitantly got out of the car, sending a worried look to her boyfriend. For some reason, she felt uneasy about writing along with the deputy. Maybe it was because she had seen some of the pictures he had taken of the missing girls and found them to be much too provocative. She didn't know who was killing her friends, but until he was caught, she wasn't taking chances with anybody but Tommy.

91

"That's a cute outfit you got on. You look just like a little porcelain doll," the Deputy said, giving her the eye.

His comments worried Darlene even more. Tommy turned the key and cranked the engine, but it refused to catch. As the Deputy headed for Darlene around the back of the vehicle, he gave the boy a look that sent shivers of fright through him. He didn't know what he could do since the deputy had a gun. And he hated leaving Darlene behind, but what could he do? Maybe if he could get out of there and tell someone, Dale would not hurt her, knowing that others would know he was last one scene with her.

Throwing open the door, Tommy flew out of the car and into the woods. Dale grinned, happy to be rid of him. Further spooked by her boyfriend's reaction, Darlene grew so leery that she began to shake.

"I don't live too far from here," she said, slipping out of the car and inching away from the Deputy. "I can walk, really."

"Can't let you do that. Get in the car," Dale ordered, his stern look making up her mind.

Running around the front of the Pinto, she escaped in the same direction as Tommy. Dale chased after, determined to catch her.

* * *

Katie carefully applied the make-up she had been given and brushed her hair, braiding it into two pigtails as ordered, all under the careful watch of her shadowed captor. She knew that if she messed up, she would be forced to remove the makeup and start all over again. For some reason, she had to do it perfectly. As she gazed at her image in the old wall mirror hanging on the wall, she couldn't help thinking that she looked just like a doll – a doll that she feared would soon look like all the other bodies they had discovered down by the creek.

"Why are you making me do this?"

When her captor did not answer, she asked more questions. "What happens to me when this is over? Are you going to kill me like all the others? You took Teresa Crawford and the other girls, too, didn't you? What number am I? Did they fight you? Did they refuse to do what you wanted? I've done everything you've asked. I've cooperated in every way. Please let me go. Please... Don't kill me."

The blade of a knife pressed against the back of Katie's neck, silencing her.

"Questions, questions, questions...Shut up! You talk too much." The voice had an almost hysterical tone to it, but it was hard to be sure through the overriding anger mixed with eager anticipation of what would happen next. And that's what it was all about...what happened next.

* * *

Lightning from an oncoming thunderstorm illuminated the interior of the Mayor's house, making the old home seem ominous and spooky. The front porch light flickered on and off like the bulb could not make up its mind whether to burn out or not. From the bushes, the three companions scanned the exterior of the building, hoping the house's occupant would not be home.

Crack!

The violent snap of thunder startled them, making them jump as Quinn scoured the area using the night vision lens she had attached to her camera. She carefully studied the driveway, porch, and surrounding yard, looking for any sign of movement. There was nothing. All the places she examined were empty, and she saw nothing more than the violent wrestling of the bushes as the wind from the oncoming storm tore at them.

"No vehicles. One light is on the inside," she whispered to the others. "Maybe he's not home."

"You two check the rear," Larry said. "I'll take the front. Let's go."

Quinn and Jamal dashed to the back of the house and hid behind some old trash cans located in the back of the property by the unattached garage. Quinn once more scanned the area with her night vision lens and sighed.

"All's clear," she said in a soft voice.

Then one of the cans moved, violently shook, and crashed to the ground with a loud clang. Quinn and Jamal jumped back, their hearts and their throats, as an opossum appeared and stuck its head back inside the trash barrel, rummaging for food.

"Gross," Quinn said, but her voice was filled with relief. "That tail makes it look like a big rat." She shivered. "And I hate rats."

Larry hunched below the windows as he passed along the front of the house, carefully peeking through each pane as he made his way from right to left. Satisfied, he crept back to the door. A flash of lightning illuminated the image of a man, startling him so badly that he nearly wet himself. He fell back, breathing hard, and prayed that he had not been spotted. Waiting several moments, he repeated a silent mantra. *Don't come out. Don't come out. Don't come out.* He crossed his fingers and fervently hoped that the Mayor would not come charging out of the house with a shotgun. When nothing happened, he finally took a deep breath and drew upon his courage. Slowly raising his head in front of the window, Larry peeked inside one more, breathing a sigh of relief

when he realized that what he had seen was nothing more than a coat and hat hanging on a wooden coat tree. *I gotta stop doing this.*

In the backyard, Jamal and Quinn felt the wind picking up and gusting as they crossed the distance between the garage and the house. When they reached their destination, they pressed their backs against the siding, its paint cracked and peeling.

"Something is scratching," Jamal whispered.

"What?" Quinn asked. When he didn't answer her right away, she turned and looked at him, a puzzled expression on her face. "What did you say?"

"It sounds like someone is scratching on something wooden…possibly a door. The girl must be trying to escape. We have to hurry up and help her."

"Shhh," Quinn said. "It's just branches rubbing against the house."

Gathering their courage, they worked their way up to the back of the house and paused to listen closely. When nothing happened, they moved further along until they reached the back door where they peered through the window.

"Nothing," Jamal said, relieved.

He carefully turned the doorknob. Surprisingly, it was unlocked, and he gave Quinn a puzzled look.

"Small town folks often don't lock their door. For some silly reason, they seem to think that because they know everyone in town, no one would dare break into their home," she whispered.

"That's ridiculous," Jamal whispered back. "Do you know how many shows I have seen of people who live in a small town, who don't lock their doors, and still end up being murdered?"

Quinn shook her head and rolled her eyes. Her expression showed that she obviously agreed with him. Jamal gently pushed on the door, and as it opened a crack, revealing a small laundry room, the light in the next room turned on. He quickly and quietly pulled the door shut, and they dove under the kitchen window. As they waited, they tried to slow their frightened breathing. Then they heard the muffled sound of chopping, the steady rhythm of a large knife or a small hatchet cutting through what had to be something thick and hard to cut before chopping into a wooden cutting board beneath.

Quinn and Jamal exchanged horrified glances, and Quinn pointed up at the window. Jamal rapidly shook his head no. If what he feared was happening, he did not want to see it. Firming her resolve, Quinn glared at him and once more jabbed her finger upward, but Jamal again shook his head. She narrowed her eyes and crossed her arms, giving him a look he often referred to as "the eye." Jamal sighed. He hated it when she did that. It made him feel uneasy whenever she looked at him that way.

Finally, when she raised her right eyebrow, he nodded, and the two friends inched up each side of the window. What they saw seemed to confirm. Jamal's worst fears and horrified them both. The Mayor was busy chopping up suspicious chunks of red meat. Quinn and Jamal gagged, fighting back waves of nausea. Suddenly, the Mayor's two dogs started barking and ran into the laundry room, where they began scratching at the wooden door. Jamal and Quinn ducked.

"Now what?" Quinn asked, horrified. Her mind tried not to think about what she thought she had just seen. They snuck another quick peek and saw the Mayor loading a crossbow. By now, the dogs were madly pawing at the door, their yips and barks increasing in fervor.

"Quick!" Jamal said. "Let's get outta here."

They only got as far as the trash cans when the back door swung open, and the two frightened friends once more ducked down behind the metal barrier, feeling exposed behind their flimsy hideout. As soon as the Mayor released the dogs, they surrounded the garbage bins, barking wildly. He scanned the yard with his flashlight and stepped away from the door. Stepping further out into the yard, he stopped a few yards from the trash cans and raised the crossbow, pointing it directly at them.

"We're dead," Quinn whispered. "Let's make a run for it."

She started to rise, but Jamal pulled her back down.

"No!" He whispered back. "We'll never make it."

An arrow whizzed through the air, piercing one of the metal cans, and stopping a mere inch from Jamal's head.

"Okay. I see your point," he said, his brown eyes large and round. "Ready…"

Another arrow whizzed past and buried itself into the ground. Instantly, the dogs stopped barking, and the flashlight turned off. A puzzled look crossed their faces as the Mayor called the dogs back inside, but only one followed him into the house. The other began sniffing around and looking for a place to do its business. Exchanging frowns, Quinn and Jamal snuck around the trash cans to a dark mound on the ground. A lightning flash revealed the dead opossum, the shaft of an arrow sticking out of its belly.

After watering the trunk of a nearby tree, the second dog ran to the front yard and cornered Larry in the bushes in front of the house. Larry pressed his body tightly against the siding and tried to inch away from the Doberman, but the dog only moved in closer.

"Damn, I hate dogs," Larry softly mumbled.

The dog cocked his head. Then seeming to understand Larry's words, he moved even closer, his barking now changing to a threatening growl that showed its gleaming fangs.

"Sorry. I didn't mean it. Nice doggy. Nice doggy."

As the animal continued to growl, Larry desperately looked around. Spotting a broken piece of branch, he grabbed it, hoping to hold back the angry Doberman, and to his amazement, the dog bit the stick and tried to pull it out of his hands. Suddenly, the porch light turned on and off as though the Mayor were flipping the switch up and down. After a moment, the bulb flickered and finally died. Larry instinctively rose up slightly and threw the stick as far as he could before ducking down again. The dog took off after it. As it did, the door opened, and the Mayor walked out, carrying a bundle of paper towels and newspapers filled with a large quantity of dripping bloody meat. Larry turned ghost white and cowered behind the bushes. *No, no, no.* Then to make matters worse, the dog reappeared, wagging its tail and holding the stick in his mouth as he waited for Larry to take and throw it again.

"Go. Scat," he frantically whispered. "Go on. Get out of here."

While the Mayor loaded his '72 station wagon with the bloody bundle, Larry threw the stick again. The sound of it hitting the ground caught the Mayor's attention. He stopped and looked to where the stick had landed. Unaware and unconcerned of the danger it was putting Larry in, the dog retrieved it once more and sprinted back into the bushes. His master slammed the back hatch of the wagon and opened the passenger door before moving closer to the bushes where Larry was hiding.

"Come on, boy, git out of them there bushes. We've got business to tend to."

Larry remained frozen in place as the dog nudged the stick closer to him with its nose, its tail furiously wagging and its tongue hanging out between excited yips.

"Come on! No time for foolin' around. I'm talking to you, boy! Come out this instant, or there will be some serious hurtin'."

Not knowing what else to do, Larry gave up and started to rise to his knees to reveal himself. At the same time, the dog turned around, jumped out of the bushes, and ran toward its master.

"Good, boy," the Mayor said, patting the animal on the head. "Now git in the car. Go on now. That's a good boy."

The dog sprinted for the open door, and the Mayor followed. After closing the passenger door, he walked around to the driver's side, got in, and drove away.

Having moved to a more concealing location, Quinn and Jamal watched the car pull away and then rose to their feet. A lightning flash revealed an old weathered shed set behind and to the left of the garage, and the two friends wondered how they had previously missed it.

"Look," Quinn said. "There's something in the shed."

Raising the camera, the night vision lens revealed what appeared to be a body hanging from the roof on a chain with a large hook. A shiny object that looked like it might be an ax appeared to be embedded in it. Quinn swallowed convulsively as fear shot through her veins, making her blood feel like it had been turned to ice. As much as she wanted to just run back to the depot and wait for the next train, she knew she had to be sure of what she thought was in the shed. But what would they do? Could they trust Sheriff Packy? She was uncertain. Nevertheless, Quinn signaled for Jamal to follow her.

As they approached the shed, the door creaked open and slammed shut to the rhythm of the brisk wind, carrying the coppery smell of blood and raw meat. Quinn peeked in the window, but it was so dirty and smeared that nothing was clear. Determined not to appear cowardly in his friend's eyes, Jamal headed for the door, and as the wind blew it open, he caught it. Covering his nose and mouth, he led Quinn inside.

As they stepped past the threshold, they were bombarded with the sickening stench, causing them to gulp the bile that threatened to rise in their throats. Multiple lightning flashes lit up the place. It looked like an old meat factory filled with bloody knives and skinned carcasses covered with flies and suspended from the ceiling on large hooks. Quinn screamed loud enough to wake the dead until a hand reached out from between the dead animals and plastered itself across her mouth, muffling the sound.

"Shhhhhhh," Larry said as he stepped out and revealed himself.

When he was sure she would not scream again, Larry removed his hand. Quinn attempted to hold back her nausea but only partially succeeded as her stomach rebelled against the ghastly sight before her.

"Are all these carcasses body parts?" Jamal asked, feeling queasy. "I think we've found the killer, but I don't know what we're going to do about it. For all we know, the Sheriff is in on it."

"Maybe, maybe not," Larry disagreed. For some reason, he did not seem to be bothered by gore around him. "These are animals, probably deer, and wild boar."

"How the hell would you know that?" Quinn asked.

Before he could answer, she ran out and promptly vomited. Jamal followed but did not get too close as he fought to get his own roiling stomach under control. Larry lingered inside the shack and studied the room. It all looks so familiar. The thing that bothered him was that the shack should be refrigerated. Why would someone go to the bother of hunting down and killing deer and other animals just to let the meat rot? It just didn't make sense.

As Jamal and Quinn fought their sickness, Larry exited the shack, clearly looking for something. When he discovered a blood trail, he called out to the others. "Hey! Check this out."

Jamal and Quinn joined him, following the trail across the lawn to a boarded-up basement window.

"She's got to be in there! It makes sense," Larry said, excited. "We've already looked in the attic, so there's no place else she could be unless..." His words trailed off as he glanced back at the shed and thought about what they had seen inside. It was animal meat...Right? Because if it wasn't, they would not find the girl inside.

Suddenly the Doberman from inside the house appeared and began barking as it pushed its way out through the doggie door. Jamal, Quinn, and Larry took off, and it ran after them. Reaching the door of the back porch first, they opened it, hurried inside, and secured the doggie door.

Thud.

Thinking it would open as it pushed through, the dog hit the door full force and bounced back.

"Yipe!"

"I really hate dogs," Larry said.

Not knowing how much time they had until the Mayor returned, Larry, Quinn, and Jamal left the laundry room and searched for the basement door. They found it in a hallway near the front foyer, but it was padlocked.

"Why would someone lock the basement door from this side?" Quinn asked. "Unless there was something inside that they didn't want to get out. She must be down there."

"Find the key or something to break it open," Larry said.

Quinn and Jamal headed into the kitchen to search. Spotting the bloody mess in the sink, they did their best to avoid looking at it. Quinn began by pulling out drawers, while Jamal searched the cupboards. She was on the second drawer when Jamal grabbed her by the shoulder. Startled, she turned to find him holding a bloody knife next to her face.

"Ahhh!" She screeched, jumping back a step. "Where did you get that?"

He nervously pointed to a bloody carcass in the sink.

"Why on earth would you pick it up?" She wrinkled her nose, telling herself that it was just more deer or boar meat. "Jamal! Don't be stupid! What if that's a murder weapon? Your fingerprints will be all over it. If the Sheriff is crooked, he could frame you for the murder."

Jamal dropped the knife as if it had suddenly grown very hot. "I'm sorry! I... I just didn't think."

"Forget that," Quinn said, shaking her head. "We need to find that key before the Mayor returns, or we may end up as his next victims."

Meanwhile, Larry searched the foyer, in the basement, a girl's hand reached out. Her nails scratched against something made of wood, making a sound similar to the one they had heard when the tree limbs were brushing against the house.

Hearing the sound, Larry stopped and listened. A crack of loud thunder tore through the house, startling everyone. It was immediately followed by a scream from downstairs.

"Screw this!" Without hesitation, Larry kicked open the door to the basement, but as it slammed into the wall, the scratching sound stopped. Everything was quiet. Maybe the girl thought the Mayor had returned.

In the kitchen, a bolt of lightning flashed through the window, and Quinn spotted the red shoe behind the pantry door. It was the same one that she had seen earlier sticking out beneath a cabinet in the dining room.

"That's it!" Quinn declared as she grabbed it. "This is the red shoe I told you about earlier."

Larry flipped the light switch, but apparently, this bulb was also burned out. He cautiously moved down the crude open staircase. The only light came from occasional streaks of lightning through the boarded-up basement windows. He slowly descended, careful not to fall down the rickety stairs. A shout of surprise escaped his lips when his ankles were grabbed from between the open steps, and he grabbed the railing to keep from falling. He struggled against the hands that threatened to pitch him forward down the staircase, but the grip on his legs was so strong that he stumbled and fell to the bottom.

Quinn heard the horrible sound of her friend tumbling down the stairs and ran through the door and down the steps, dropping the shoe at the top. As she rushed to Larry's side, Jamal screamed. He was scared witless when he noticed the Mayor's face pressed against the kitchen window and peering inside. Patrick Farlow was soaking wet, and his appearance made him look psychotic. Leaving the window, the Mayor ran to the back door and unlocked it, kicking it open and picked, causing it to slam against the wall.

Unaware of what was happening above, Larry discovered a girl hiding in the corner under the stairs. Their eyes met, but because she didn't recognize him as someone she knew, she shied away. He dashed to her side, Quinn following closely behind.

"Hold on," Larry said, keeping his voice calm and soothing. "It's okay. We're here to rescue you. Come on, we're gonna get you out of here."

"I'm scared!" The girl whined.

"No time for that," Larry said. "We have to get out of here before the Mayor returns, or we'll all be in trouble."

As he pulled her to her feet, neither he nor Quinn noticed her reach toward the plethora of broken dolls lying on a narrow, makeshift bed. The kidnapped girl clutched one to her breast as she followed him and Quinn up the steps. When they reached the foyer, they spotted the Mayor in the kitchen, holding Jamal prisoner at the point of a very large gun. The girl opened her mouth to scream, but Larry covered her mouth with his hand, and they quickly retreated around the corner.

Unfortunately, the Mayor heard the muffled scream, followed by footsteps and the slam of the front door.

"Damn it! Come back here!"

Forgetting Jamal, he rushed out the door and threw it open to see Larry, Quinn, and the girl running away in the distance.

"Hold up! Come back!" the Mayor shouted. "You don't understand!"

Jamal grabbed the red shoe and bolted out the back door, losing himself in the nearby woods.

Livid, the Mayor hopped in his car and sped off after the girl and the other Yankees. While speeding wildly after them, his hand shuffled around the backseat until he found his crossbow.

"Perfect."

Chapter Ten

The three fugitives put as much distance as possible between themselves and the Mayor's house. To make things worse, it began to rain as they slipped into the woods. Larry and Quinn pulled the girl along at a good clip until she started struggling, trying to break away from the grip they had on her arms. A moment later, she started screaming and flailing, thoroughly confusing her rescuers.

"What are you doing?" Larry asked. "Stop screaming. Stop struggling. We're trying to help you escape."

Shaking Quinn off, the girl acted like she was out of her mind, and Larry had to practically wrestle her to maintain his grip on her arm. He feared that if he let her go, she would run off and either get lost or end up running straight into her captor's arms. Hearing the scream, the Mayor stepped on the gas and raced toward the spot he thought he would find them.

Quinn's expression grew alarmed, and she pointed toward the road where the Mayor's car was bearing down on them. "Hurry, he's coming!"

"Move!" Larry snarled at the girl.

Spotting a hill that led down and off the road, he and Quinn pulled the struggling girl along. The speeding car narrowly missed hitting them. The Mayor slammed on the brakes, skidding to a stop several car lengths ahead. Then he backed up. Seeing her jailor's vehicle temporarily jarred, the girl loose from whatever internal nightmare she was having. The fugitives ran stumbling down the hill together, dodging trees and bushes as they skirted through the woods not far from the side of the road.

Shifting back into drive, Mayor Farlow flicked on his powerful flashlight and used it to track them as he followed along on the road.

"We've gotta get out of sight," Quinn gasped between breaths.

"Good idea," Larry agreed.

The three escapees ran a little further and then dove into some bushes, but as soon as they were out of sight, the girl began to struggle once more. When the Mayor no longer saw their running figures, he slammed on the brakes and skidded to a halt on the dirt road. Throwing the car into park, he threw open the door and jumped out. Watching from their hiding place in the bushes, Larry and the others didn't see him until he finally emerged from a cloud of billowing white exhaust smoke. Larry held the fidgeting girl in his arms, covering her mouth with his hand, in case she decided to start screaming again. Wondering what was going on, Quinn eyed her suspiciously. The girl had said she was afraid. So, why wouldn't she voluntarily remain quiet and still when the Mayor was so close?

"Come on out of there! I just want the girl," the Mayor called. "This isn't what you think. Just bring the girl out, and you can live to go home on the train in the morning. Nobody needs to know anything about this."

Larry put his lips to the girl's ear. "Shh, don't say a word!"

Hearing some rustling in the bushes, the Mayor lifted his crossbow and fired.

Whoosh!

The arrow flew straight and true, pinning a section of Larry's shirt to the tree next to him. Larry pulled away, ripping off part of his shirt. He and the girls ducked down as they made their way to behind some bushes further away.

107

"I've lived through this scene already," Quinn whispered. "He's a liar, and he's good with that crossbow. Let's get out of here."

"No," Larry objected as the girl finally settled down once more. "Just do what I tell you and get under these leaves."

They scooted down a small embankment approximately four feet lower than the rise above them and buried themselves in a thick pile of leaves. Thinking that the rustling came from the three trying to escape, the Mayor worked his way closer and unknowingly stood above the place where they hid. One step closer and his foot would land on Quinn's hand, which was resting under the leaves near his foot. The woods grew quiet, except for the sound of crickets and a few frogs.

The Mayor scanned the darkness, looking for deeper shadows that might belong to the fugitives. He was about to take that step, but lifted the flashlight instead, shining it around the area, even up into the branches of nearby trees. He saw nothing. As badly as he wanted to get the girl back, it was too dark to do a proper search by himself.

"If that's the way you want it, fine," he shouted. "You go on and run if you think it'll do any good. But I'll be back...," he said, smiling wickedly, "...with the dogs.

He turned and began the trek back up the hill, his feet passing near Larry's head, which was barely covered in the leaves. As he drew closer to the spot where Larry had stood earlier, he stopped and scanned the area once more, waiting to see if his threat had any effect. When nothing happened, he walked over to the tree where his arrow was embedded. He removed it and ripped off the piece of shirt that was still attached to it. Then he stuffed the fabric into his pocket and drove away.

Once the car had roared to life and left, Larry and the others stood up, brushing the dry leaves and twigs from their clothing. Larry scanned the far stretch of woods before him, seeing little more than shadows upon shadows. He then looked at the girl, who seemed dazed and in some kind of trance.

"Are you okay?" He asked.

"I'm fine, Larry," Quinn replied, giving him a dirty look. She was clearly aggravated that all his concern seemed to be for the girl with none left over for her.

The girl did not respond. She simply stared blankly at nothing.

"Come on," Larry said, finally acknowledging Quinn's presence. "We have to keep going and hope that Jamal escaped and found the Sheriff. I just hope he's legit and wants to help. Otherwise, we're in deep trouble."

Grabbing the girl by the arm again, Larry began to leave her way when she once more exploded, struggling violently and mumbling something incoherent.

"It's okay," Quinn soothed. "Jamal will find the Sheriff. Then everything will be all right." Under her breath, she said, "Or at least I hope it will."

The girl turned and stared at her strangely. Then inexplicably, she smiled and reached out. She stroked Quinn's hair, calming noticeably. Neither Larry nor Quinn knew what to make of this reaction. They found it weird, but they were thankful that the girl finally decided to come with them peacefully.

* * *

At the Sheriff's office, Packy pinned Teresa's photo to the wall, matching it up with the crime scene picture. The photos and their locations on the map formed a linear pattern along a creek and connected with the railroad track. He was so lost in thought that the sound of the door opening startled him, and he turned to find Bernadette holding a dish covered with a red and white checkered kitchen towel.

"I figured you'd be here," she said, smiling as she pulled away the towel to reveal a hot apple pie just out of the oven. It smelled delicious.

Packy was stunned. "Wow... that's really kind of you. You remembered that it's my favorite. Thanks, Bernadette."

"Can I have a piece?" The prisoner asked, licking his lips.

"Sure, Earl," Bernadette replied.

After going home, Earl had gone into an argument with his wife. She kicked him out. With nowhere else to go, he headed back to the Sheriff's office and settled into his cell. Although this time, the door was not locked.

Pulling paper plates and plastic forks from the cupboard, Bernadette cut two pieces of pie, handing one to Packy and passing the other piece to Earl, who had left his cell to join them.

"You're killing yourself, working like this," she told Packy as he settled into the chair behind his desk.

"I'm not the one doing the killing around here," Packy replied.

"That's right," Earl said after chewing and swallowing a large bite of the warm fruity dessert. "He's trying to stop him, especially since yer daughter's now involved. Thanks a heap for the pie, Bernadette. This is right tasty."

He wandered back to his cell and settled down on the bunk, where he continued to consume the dessert.

His words hit Bernadette like a ton of bricks, and her expression grew alarmed. "Excuse me? Packy? He's got, Katie? Are you certain?"

"Shut up, Earl!" Packy growled. "Don't listen to him, Bernadette. He's drunk and doesn't know what he's talking about. I have no idea if Katie's been taken or not. As far as we know, she's somewhere safe and just doesn't realize what a fuss she's causing."

"Sheriff's been real busy putting Katie on the missing girls' list," Earl continued as though he hadn't heard a word Packy had said. "Been callin' folks and doing searches all over. Yep, doing a stand-up job, I'd say. Deserving of a kiss…" His eyebrows bounced up and down in expectation.

Bernadette marched around the desk and slapped the Sheriff across the face so hard that it left a bright red imprint of her hand. "You're a real son-of-a-bitch, you know that? You had clues. You knew she was the next one, and you kept it a secret from me, told me not to jump to conclusions. How can I ever trust you again if I can't believe what you say? You're falling apart, Packy."

"I wanted to fix this without worrying you," the Sheriff said, shame-faced. "I hate to see you in pain."

"Sometimes, you can't fix everything by yourself, Packy." Her voice softened. "Life is bigger than that. We need each other. I know that now, but it doesn't help when you keep secrets from me, especially when they involve my daughter."

"I can't let this beat me." Packy laid down his fork and looked at her, his expression was morose.

"This isn't just about the missing girls anymore, is it?" Bernadette asked. "When are you gonna let your wife go? That accident wasn't your fault. These murders aren't your fault either! They're happening, and the only thing you can do is try to catch this madman."

"That's easy for you to say. Your child didn't die in your arms as your spouse lay dead in the front seat, and you don't have to pin these missing girls' pictures to the wall and stare at their faces every day, knowing they'll never smile, never kiss another boy, and never have the life they've been cheated out of."

He removed a picture of his daughter from the middle desk drawer and stared at it until Bernadette snatched it from his fingers.

"And I suppose you think it's easy for me when my daughter is one of the missing and probably this killer's next victim."

"No, Bernadette. Lord no. This isn't easy for any of us."

Anger infused her cheeks once more, and she snatched the whiskey flask from the top of his desk. "If you continue like this, you're not going to be able to help anyone."

She stormed out, taking the flask with her.

"See," Earl said. "Ya should've kissed her."

* * *

Jamal ran up to Shaky Pete's, hoping he would find the Sheriff inside.

Pete was on the phone, his patrons still sitting around drinking, playing pool, spitting tobacco, and jawing when Jamal rushed in. The sound level ratcheted down several decimals, and every eye in the place seemed to follow him as he hurried across the room. There was some murmuring and snickering among the patrons, but Jamal remained firm under their stares and marched right up to Pete.

"Where's the Sheriff?" Jamal asked.

"Come on, get outta here. I don't want any trouble," Pete said, covering the receiver with his hand. "You've caused enough problems already."

"There's an emergency," Jamal insisted. "I need the sheriff."

A couple of brawlers, much bigger than Jamal, approached the bar and stood on either side of him.

"Didn't you hear the man?" the lead brawler asked. His expression clearly stated that he was looking for a fight. "It's time to leave, city boy."

Seeing that he was surrounded, Jamal grew nervous, but he was determined to find help for his friends and the girl they had rescued. To his way of thinking, his friends were now facing the same danger as the girl. However, in their case, he figured that the mayor would forget the torture and just outright murdered them.

"What's that?" Pete said into the phone. "One just walked in. You got it. Don't you worry. We'll take care of it."

He hung up the phone.

"Look. We're in trouble and need help. The Mayor tried to kill us when we rescued that girl we told you about. I'd go to the Sheriff, but we think he's in on it, too."

Shaky Pete nodded and signaled the patrons. Several more left their chairs and encircled Jamal.

"Well now, I'd have to say that you're right on every count. You are indeed in trouble, and the Sheriff is in on it. Tell me where the girl is, and you just might live long enough to get on that train in the mornin'. Don't dilly dally, Yankee You get one chance to answer, and you'd better be telling the truth."

Jamal swallowed hard. Fear made his throat feel like it had just closed up. "I don't know. I swear! I'm guessing she's somewhere out there with my friends, but I have no idea which way they went. They ran out before I did."

"Wrong answer," Pete said, shaking his head and turning to the men surrounding the unfortunate Jamal. "Wilson, you and Jake see if you can 'flush' it out of him. Luke, Hank, Leonard, Butch, Harrison and Billy, get on over to the Mayor's and see what you can do to help, but first, go fetch yer dogs. One way or another, we've got to find them."

Wilson and Jake dragged the struggling Jamal toward the restroom, while a flurry of drunken bar patrons barreled out of Shaky Pete's, hollering and working themselves into what they felt was a righteous fury. They peeled out in their pickup trucks and headed over to the Mayor's house.

Chapter Eleven

The Sheriff's Jeep pulled into the driveway of a small, two-story house with white siding and dark green shutters. Leaving his vehicle, Packy walked up to the front door and knocked. Moments passed, and after knocking a second time, Deputy Dale finally answered, blocking the doorway so that the Sheriff could not come inside.

"Hey, Sheriff."

"Hey, Dale. Just came to check in with ya. See if you saw anything while you were on duty tonight." Packy noticed his deputy's nervousness and wondered about it. Was he hiding something inside that he didn't want the Sheriff to see?

"Uh, no... No word on Katie. Jason's at home. He claims he hasn't seen her since he left her house earlier in the evening. You hear anything?"

"Nope. Breaking for lunch?"

"Uh...no. I've got to quit early tonight. I think I'm coming down with the flu."

Packy carefully studied his deputy's face. Dale did not look sick to him. "Why didn't you call and let me know? You know, I want someone on duty at all times, especially with this killer on the loose."

"Uh...I was just about to call you," the deputy said lamely.

"By any chance, did you happen to see Darlene Tucker or Tommy Wallace while you were up on the parkway? Gotta call from her father. He said the two of them had gone out earlier."

"No one was up there, but I did see Tommy's car abandoned by the roadside. He must've had car trouble. I'm sure they're okay, though."

"I'm not so certain. Neither one has made it home yet, and their parents are pretty worried."

"They're probably just making out somewhere and forgot the time," the Deputy replied. It was all he could do not to glance back over his shoulder.

"For Tommy's sake, I hope you're wrong about that. Darlene's father will skin him alive. Anyway, I really need you to work with me all night. We have to find them. I just hope they didn't end up being snatched like Katie."

"Well," the deputy said with a sigh, "I don't know. My guts are really churning."

"Take some Imodium. That'll fix you up right quick, and by the way, I'm in no mood for Barry Manilow music tonight."

Dale shook his head. "Sorry. I don't think I could keep the medicine down, so I'd better stay close to the john."

The Sheriff hesitated. He eyed Dale suspiciously, before turning and leaving. As soon as his car was out of sight, Dale opened the door of the coat closet, revealing Darlene and Tommy huddled inside.

"You were very smart not to make a sound."

* * *

The rain finally subsided, and the wind died down to a breeze. Larry continued to lead Quinn and the girl along the highway, trying to get this far away from the Mayor as possible. He knew that if Farlow came back with his dogs, it would make it a lot more difficult for them to escape capture.

"You okay?" He asked the girl. "What's your name?"

The girl's name was Mary Jo, but for some reason, she had trouble speaking or understanding what he wanted. Instead of answering his question, she said, "I stay in that room...always."

"Her thoughts are probably scrambled right now," Quinn said. "After what she's been through, she's probably terrified out of her mind."

"You could be right," there he agreed.

"What are we going to do about Jamal?"

"I'm pretty sure he got away from the Mayor," Larry answered. "I saw him running for the railroad tracks, right before we ducked into the woods, and since we're the ones being chased, he's probably okay."

"Shouldn't we go that way?" Quinn asked, pointing toward the railroad tracks. "If we do, we should run into him."

Mary Jo pointed to a spot deeper into the woods. Apparently, she was familiar with this area. "There. I go this way."

"Fine," Quinn said. "Just get us out of here."

As they made their way through the thick underbrush and into the dense woods, Larry stumbled over something moving along the ground and fell on something small and squiggly. It let out a horrible sound.

Squeak!

Larry rose to his knees, and a wild piglet scooted away into the brush, squealing in fear. Several more stood nearby. Startled, he jumped to his feet, but as he did, he heard a grunting noise behind him. Quinn and Mary Jo turned to see a huge wild sow, which apparently was the piglets' mother. And, she was fighting mad. In an effort to protect her babies, she snorted and charged after them.

"Run!" Larry shouted.

The three humans scattered, trying to put as much distance as possible between themselves and the sharp tusks of the angry sow, which chased them a few yards before coming to a halt. Satisfied with scaring off the enemy, the momma returned, dropped to the ground, and started nursing her piglets as if nothing had happened. It was nature's way of calming the distressed piglets.

* * *

Back in the restroom at Shaky Pete's, Wilson and Jake dunked Jamal's head in the grimy swirling water of the toilet for what seemed like the hundredth time.

"I'll tell ya what," Wilson said in his most persuasive voice. "The next drink is on me. Just tell me where the girl is."

"I swear! I don't know," Jamal sputtered. "I never even saw her!"

"Too bad," Wilson replied. "Bottom's up!"

Jake dunked Jamal's head back into the toilet water, while Wilson sat on him.

* * *

Meanwhile, the Sheriff drove toward town, passing a caravan of pick-up trucks going in the opposite direction. "That's odd," he said aloud. "I wonder where the boys are off to at this time of night. Strange, it looks like they might be headin' for the Mayor's house."

* * *

In the bathroom, Jamal was pulled out of the dunk.

"Do ya feel like talkin' now?" Jake asked.

Jamal was practically in tears, his voice begging them to believe him. "I'm telling you. I don't know where she is. I swear!"

Jake shook his head. "Let's make this one a double, Wilson."

The city boy's head was shoved into the swirling toilet water twice more, pinned by Wilson' butt so that he could not jerk upward. Jamal nearly gagged when the nasty aroma of a beer fart blasted next to his ear.

* * *

At the Mayor's house, the convoy of pickup trucks spun gravel as they pulled up. The men with their dogs spilled out, surrounding the Mayor's old van.

"We're here to help," the men called when they spotted Patrick Farlow bringing his dogs out the front door.

"Thanks, boys, we don't have a lot of options left, I'm afraid. They're headed into the woods."

The Mayor held up the piece of Larry's shirt that had been torn off by his arrow. He gave each of the dogs a good whiff. They immediately began howling and barking and took off, their noses to the ground, knowing exactly where to go.

* * *

Further away, Larry searched everywhere for a path but wasn't having any luck finding one. If he could find even in the old animal trail, they would be able to make better time.

"What now, whatever your name is?" He asked Mary Jo.

"I go this way," she said.

"Back off and give her a break," Quinn said, scowling. "It is dark out here."

In the distance, the sound of barking dogs and shouting men filled the air.

"Here come the dogs. That sure didn't take long," Larry complained. Locating some moss on one of the trees, Larry looked at the lit face of his watch and then checked the position of the stars and full moon above. "North is over there. Come on."

* * *

Back at the bar, things were unusually quiet in the sparsely occupied room as the Sheriff came through the front door. Pete poured a beer and placed it on the bar in front of him.

"Not tonight, Pete." Packy looked around, growing suspicious. "What's going on here? You and the boys are up to something. I just saw a whole convoy heading for the Mayor's house."

"Not to worry, Sheriff. Everything is under control."

Packy looked about the room, noting that the remaining patrons nervously eyed the bathroom door. He headed for the restroom, but three large patrons intercepted him, blocking the way.

"You don't need to go in there. We know how to handle family business proper-like Sheriff," a well-built man by the name of Duke said as he took a firm stance and folded his arms across his chest.

Packy looked at Pete.

"This involves us, too," Pete added.

Convinced that something bad was happening, the Sheriff pushed through the three men. They tried to stop him, putting up a half-hearted fight, but it didn't last long.

Packy took Duke with a swift kick in the groin. He then immobilized the other two with a simple "thumb lock" and shoved them aside.

In the restroom, Jamal gasped for breath, his head and shirt drenched. Wilson and Jake howled with laughter.

"I'll bet he won't talk cause he thinks we don't like him," Wilson said. "I say we give him a *Deliverance* smooch and let him know he's pretty. Maybe he'll talk then."

Jake chuckled, but then gave Jamal a sobering look. "Just kiddin'. We don't really do that kinda thing."

"Oh yes, we do," Wilson argued.

There was an awkward moment before the door burst open. Wilson moved to block the Sheriff's entrance, but before he could put up much of a fight, a pool stick was cracked over his head. He passed out. Packy continued into the restroom and grabbed Jake's ear, twisting it painfully. Jamal quickly pulled his head from the toilet.

"It wasn't my idea," Jake whined. "I had nothing to do with it."

"Get up!" Packy shouted as he pulled Jamal to his feet.

* * *

Still trekking through the woods, the trio approached what seemed to be a kerosene lamp, hanging in a nearby clearing. They moved closer and found a rickety, rust-ridden trailer surrounded by weeds and being held up, or so it seemed, by what appeared to be a myriad of junk. Alerted to their presence, an old Labrador retriever started barking from inside the trailer, and the three fugitives quickly hid behind a large boulder.

Bang!

121

Larry and the others nearly jumped out of their skin when a blind old hag came out of the trailer with the dog and fired a rifle into the air. The three huddled behind their hiding place.

"Is everybody around here crazy?" Larry whispered.

Deeper in the woods, the Mayor halted the posse at the sound of the distant gunshot. Knowing where it had to have come from, he smiled and pointed to the left. "This way, boys, we've got em now!"

The men headed off in the new direction.

* * *

After rescuing Jamal, Sheriff Packy returned to his office. Although, not before pulling over and arresting another drunk driver. He locked the man up, and poured himself a mug of black coffee. Taking a sip, he set it down and walked over to his desk, where he pulled out a drawer and retrieved the pictures of the missing girls. All of them were pretty, but that's where the similarities stopped. As far as he could tell, there was absolutely no connection between them. They varied in age from twelve to seventeen. Some had short hair, some long, and the colors varied between brown, blonde, red, and black. Pictures of the dead girls' bodies showed the different locations along the creek, where they had been discovered. Packy sadly ruminated over the pictures.

Earl was asleep in his cell, as the drunken man pressed his face to the bars and called out.

"He's still out there, Sheriff! He ain't through yet."

Packy tried to ignore him.

"You ain't getting any closer to catching him, and you know it! Two years this has been going on, and you're still no closer."

Annoyed, Packy looked up at the man, unappreciative of the comment. "Quiet down."

"I know what you're thinking, but I ain't him!"

The Sheriff hadn't really considered the man as a suspect, but as he thought about it, he wondered. "You've been living alone these past two years."

"And you've been living alone, too, since your wife died a couple of years ago, but you're not behind bars."

The Sheriff studied the girl's pictures. "I need you to be quiet."

"Come on, Sheriff! Let me outta here!"

Packy gave Earl a funny look and ignored the man as he looked over the pictures until Jamal entered the station a few moments later.

"I can't believe what I am seeing," the Sheriff growled. "What part of 'stay at the depot' confused you?" Packy asked. His voice was filled with annoyance. "Where are your friends?"

Words began to flow from Jamal's mouth like an unchecked waterfall, making little sense. "I don't know, but we need your help. We found the kidnapped girl! Quinn spotted a lady's shoe at the Mayor's house. I distinctly remember him saying that he hadn't had a woman there in years. We went back to his house and...and...the Mayor...he had a gun...and a crossbow! And there was an opossum in the trash. It scared us, but he shot it. We thought... we thought he was shooting at us. And then we heard this scratching on the outside, but it was just the wind blowing some branches against the

123

house! But then, there was scratching on the inside of the house, and…we knew it couldn't be the wind this time. Oh, and the red shoe…I found it."

He pulled the red shoe out of his pocket and was about to place it on the Sheriff's desk when the Sheriff yelled at him.

"Stop!" Packy's voice was so stern that Jamal pocketed the shoe, and his mouth closed with a snap. "Where's the girl now?"

"I don't know. I got separated from the others, and I didn't see which way they were headed," Jamal replied. "Those guys back at the bar were trying to make me tell them where she is, but I don't know! Really!"

"Did you see her?"

"No. The Mayor was going to kill us! We gotta get over there before Larry, Quinn, and the girl end up murdered, just like the others, but where could they be?" Jamal asked.

"They could've gone to a couple places, but I don't think they'd be welcome at either. Folks 'round here protect their own and don't like strangers. They got ways of scaring 'em off, which was probably all the Mayor was trying to do. Scare you off."

Jamal turned to him, angry. "You're wrong. He knew we had the girl, and he was trying to kill us. What is it with the people in this town? You're all freakin' nuts!"

"You don't know nothin' about this town or its people, so watch your mouth!"

"I know enough. For crying out loud, we were just trying to help someone," Jamal said. "And you haven't been much better. You've been giving us grief every step of the way. Don't you even care that more people may die?"

"Of course, I care!" Packy shouted.

His outburst was so emotional that Jamal closed his mouth with a snap, leaving what he was about to say unsaid.

"I can't close my eyes at night without seeing those girls' faces staring at me with sightless eyes or watching their mothers crying over their daughters' graves. It breaks my heart that I can't find the monster that's doing this. So, don't you tell me for one minute that I don't care, because I do!"

Jamal sat straighter. "The monster is the Mayor! Why can't you see that?"

"I know it looks like Patrick…but dammit…it isn't him. You city slickers think you've got it all figured out, don't you? Think you can breeze in here and give us all the answers, but you don't even know what the question is. Things aren't what they appear to be." Realizing that he was yelling as the boy, he softened. "This town's hurtin' on account of what's been going on. We don't need you judging us and pretending like you know it all."

* * *

The Mayor, his men, and the sniffing dogs continued their hunt through the woods, hot on the trail of Larry, Quinn, and Mary Jo. Back at the trailer, an old hag fired again. Several yards away, a raccoon fell dead and hit the ground with a thud.

"Did I get 'em?" She asked the dog.

It barked and ran into the underbrush.

Larry stood up within eyesight of her and waved his arms. The old hag stared right at him and squinted, but her eyes were both covered with cataracts, making it next to impossible to see. She raised her shotgun, pointing at his chest and pulled back the hammer.

125

"Wait! Stop!" Larry pleaded. "I need help."

"Who's there? I can't see ya. I'm warnin' ya, I just killed a raccoon at twenty yards. I can hear ya just fine, but I don't recognize yer voice, so don't test me."

"Don't shoot, and please don't have your dog attack," Larry said. "I need help."

The dog retrieved the dead animal and returned to her, his tail wagging. She lowered the gun and extended her hand for the prize, grinning a gapped-tooth smile when the Labrador pushed the raccoon against her questing fingers.

"Ah, hah! Good dog," she hooted. "That's some good eatin'! Well, come on up then. I ain't gonna shoot ya…maybe." She cackled. "Come on now."

She beckoned them forward, and the three fugitives cautiously emerged from their hiding place. As they moved closer, the hag faked an attack, and all three jumped. She laughed, faked it again, and got the same response. She continued laughing, but then she grew suspicious. "You alone?"

"Are you blind or what?" Quinn asked sarcastically.

"Course I'm blind," she snarled. "Any fool can see that."

Quinn blushed to the roots of her hair. "Sorry."

"What business you got out here?" The old hag asked. "Most folks know better than to come snooping around out here."

"We're lost. I've got two girls with me, and we're in a lot of trouble."

"Sounds like yer lucky day," the hag laughed. "What kind of trouble?"

"We're being chased by the Mayor," Larry answered. "He tried to kill us with the crossbow."

As he finished speaking, the old woman heard the hounds barking in the distance.

126

"Quick! Git' in here. Any enemy of the Mayor is a friend of mine. My name's Ethel!"

Chapter Twelve

Larry, Quinn, and Mary Jo followed the old hag into her trailer. She dropped the supposedly dead raccoon onto the kitchen table, but as it hit the wooden surface, the animal twitched. A startled Larry backed away, looking disgusted. He tried not to throw up in revulsion, which was odd since being around all that butchered meat hadn't made him nauseous. Looking around, he and the others noticed that the trailer was filled with every kind of knickknack the old woman had found over the years in the trash, along with the smells that accompanied them.

"Sounds like he's got dogs after ya," Ethel cackled as she rapped the raccoon on the head with a meat tenderizer hammer, just to make sure it was dead. "Must be serious."

"Yes, ma'am," Larry replied. "I believe it is. The Mayor isn't the nice, community-minded person people think he is. He's got secrets, terrible secrets."

"Too bad, you can't stay for dinner. I make a mighty fine raccoon stew." She started rummaging around in her cabinets, counting off things while she talked. "We all knew it. Never agreed with it, but we always knew he was up to no good. I never liked that Mayor. I have a sense about people, but I feel there is something right about you. Are you from around here?"

"Hell no," Larry replied a bit too vehemently, drawing a curious yet startled look from Quinn.

"I believe you're telling me the truth. The Mayor, however, is another kinda critter. I never got a good sense from him, not ever. I always felt there was more to the story. He was dishin' out to everyone. Mark my words. Given time, the truth is always revealed."

Setting down the stuff she retrieved, the old lady started acting crazy, walking in circles as she set things on the table and talked to them. "Take your shirt off."

"What?" Larry blurted.

"Take it off. Hurry up now. I gotta use it as a decoy."

"Take hers," Larry complained.

"If you think I'm going to run around in my bra, you've got another thing coming," Quinn angrily protested.

"You should be ashamed. Ain't no never mind for you, boy. I'll bet you got a t-shirt underneath those fancy duds you're wearing," she said as she ran her gnarled fingers over the silky material of his shirt.

"She can wear my t-shirt. This cost me $300," Larry insisted.

The old woman brandished a knife and skillfully cut off his shirt in one neat, efficient slice.

"Not with that anymore," she laughed. "What's more important, boy, your $300 shirt, or your life?"

Scowling, Larry removed his ruined shirt and handed it to Ethel. She used it to dress up her dog.

"How's he look?" Ethel asked. "You know I can't see. Ha!"

Larry stepped back. He had forgotten about her blindness and wondered how she managed to slice up his shirt without cutting him in the process.

Ethel smacked the dog's hindquarters and walked out onto her front porch, sending the Doberman off into the woods.

"Go on, girl," she cackled. "Go find yerself a male dog, maybe two like this boy. Make some puppies. Go on." She grabbed a can and shook it, dancing around. "Come on out here, boy," she called.

Larry and the others joined her on the porch.

"You," Ethel said, pointing to Larry. "Run around the back of the house to the first few feet in the woods." As she spoke, the sound of barking dogs grew louder. "Then return here, but make sure you stay on the same path."

"I don't understand," Larry said.

"The dogs will follow the scent," she explained.

Larry ran to the woods behind the house and back. When he returned, he found the old lady shaking pepper on the floor and the stoop and just inside her door.

"There," she said, straightening up. "We're almost done. The dogs will follow the scent of yer shirt. Yer city folk ain't ya? Ya'll is dumb as doornails. Nice, but senseless. Now, we've only got one problem. What do I do with the three of you? I've got to hide you someplace they will find ya."

* * *

To Jamal's surprise, the Sheriff gave him a hard shove into one of his two jail cells and locked the door.

"Hey!" Jamal shouted. "What's going on? I'm not the killer, and neither are my friends!"

"I know," the Sheriff replied. "I asked you to stay at the train depot, but you wouldn't listen. So I'm putting you in there for your own good."

"You can't do this! We're here to help!"

"Don't need your help. I'm the Sheriff," Packy replied. "This will keep you out of trouble and out of my way. You kids don't know what you've done! Nothing is what it seems. You should have left when I told you. Given the situation, your friends might as well be dead. And with that fired up a bunch of drunken heehaws after them, their lives are in grave danger."

"So, they will kill them?" Jamal's questions sounded more like a statement.

"They won't mean to, but things being as they are, the situation could easily get out of hand."

* * *

Searching the deep woods, the men could barely keep up with their barking dogs. Since they weren't following a path, the Mayor and his posse had to work their way through thick brush and fallen branches, and occasionally, someone would trip over a tree root that was sticking out too far. Eventually, the Mayor and his motley crew broke through the bushes and found the dogs going ballistic in front of Ethel's trailer.

The Mayor smirked and turned to his men. "Stay here, boys. I'll handle this."

He marched up the wooden steps of the porch that had been attached to the side of the trailer and banged his fist on the door. "Open up, Ethel! You know why I'm here. What have you seen?"

"Nothing fer the past twenty-three years," she replied with a snicker.

"You're not funny, Ethel. You know what I mean," the Mayor insisted.

"Oh yeah, I know what you mean, Mayor. I know more than you think I know. I see things other folks don't see. And I'm not afraid to speak my mind either." The door opened, and Ethel appeared. "Good to see you, Mayor. You've looked better."

"Cut the crap, Ethel. I know you don't like me, but you got something of mine in there, and I want it back. So be quick about it and fetch them youngins out here, or I'll have to start playing rough."

He shoved the woman aside, causing her to fall against the side of the trailer. Then he forced his way inside, carrying his crossbow and looking around. After a cursory glance, he poked his head back through the door.

"Search the place!" The Mayor shouted to his men. "They've got to be in here somewhere!"

The Mayor's men ransacked her property, but when one of the dogs tried to cross the threshold, it began violently sneezing. The dog's owner looked down, and seeing the profusion of black flakes on the floor, he gave her a nasty look.

"The old hag must have sprinkled pepper by the door here, Mayor. Old Jezebel is sneezing her head off."

"Ha! So you *are* hiding them in here," the Mayor accused her.

"Am not! I put that there to keep wild animals from wandering inside and upsetting my Tula Belle."

"I'll just bet. And just where is your Tula Belle?"

"Out and about," Ethel chuckled. "Better watch your dogs. Could be she's in heat."

132

The mayor ignored her words and turned to his posse of men. "Boys, toss everything outside, starting with her if you have to. I want them kids found!"

One of the men was about to shove the old lady outside when the dogs picked up the scent in the backyard and started barking, pulling their masters toward the woods.

"They're over here!" Butch shouted. "We found them."

"You did?" The old woman anxiously asked as she followed the Mayor outback.

"They took off that away," Butch said excitedly. "The dogs got the scent."

As the Mayor hurried around back, the old woman grabbed his arm.

"You've messed up my place!"

"Trust me, Ethel. It doesn't look any different," the Mayor said as he and his men ran after their dogs.

"Yer going to pay fer yer secrets, Mayor," the old woman shouted after them. "Mark my words. I know what they be!"

The Mayor stopped and opened his mouth to reply, but he was interrupted by Butch.

"Don't pay that old biddy no, never mind. She's crazy as a loon. Ain't no one gonna listen to anything she has to say. Let's go, Mayor."

They took off after the dogs.

Ethel waited in the back yard until the sound of the dog's baying grew softer in the distance. Nodding her head once, she headed for the outhouse and opened the door as if she had 'business' to do. All three renegades huddled on top of each other over the smelly bench with a hole in the center. Larry and Quinn were pinching their nostrils closed, but apparently, the smell didn't seem to bother Mary Jo.

"They're gone, but they will figure it out soon enough. You'd better get going. Take this pepper can and head down that path over there," she said, pointing to the left. "It'll take you to the creek. Follow it down to the mill. After that, it'll take you directly into town."

"Thank you for your help, ma'am, I don't know what we would have done without you," Larry said.

* * *

The Sheriff headed for the door, intent on tracking down the mob and stopping this insanity before someone ended up dead.

"Wait! Come back, please," Jamal shouted. "Please, they're my friends. We were just trying to help."

Packy reached for the doorknob and turned it, but before he took a step outside, he returned to the cell and released Jamal.

"This is against my better judgment, but you can come. However, you had better do what I tell ya, or next time, I'll lock you up until the train arrives in the mornin'."

Relieved, as soon as the Sheriff opened the door, Jamal hurried from the cell. "I will. I swear. I'll do whatever you say."

They hurried to the Jeep and drove off, but had little luck finding the three fugitives or the posse. After driving two complete circuits around town and the outlying areas, the excitement of the chase began to die down. It seemed like they would never find Larry or the others, and Jamal began to wonder if they were already too late.

Looking around at the dilapidated buildings, Jamal asked, "What happened here?"

Packy took a moment, thinking it through before answering. "The mine and mill were closed down within weeks of each other, and that pretty much did everyone in. People lost their jobs, their homes, just about everything they had. They gave up. Can't rightly say I blame them."

"What about you?" Jamal asked.

"I was born here, but when I was four, I was sent to live with my aunt in Chicago. My mother was very ill, and she was unable to take care of the three of us. Since my half-brother was a lot older, he stayed behind with my dad to help care for her and my little sister, who was also sickly. In Chicago, life was a whole lot easier, although I missed my family. My aunt put me through the University. After that, I went to work for the FBI, and I had no intention of ever coming back here, except maybe to visit. Then one day unexpectedly, my father was killed when his tractor flipped over on top of him, and mom got sicker. That was four years ago. I moved my family here to care for her, but with my dad gone, I think she just gave up. She died a year later. Thing is, I knew as soon as I moved back that this wasn't my hometown anymore. I just didn't fit in. Billy is the only person to move here since I came back."

"I thought he didn't look like a local," Jamal said.

"Don't be fooled by him. Billy grew up in Maine, went to an Ivy League college, and graduated with a Ph.D. As soon as he received his doctorate, he went overseas to work as a missionary. Billy's something special. He's the kind of man that tempts me to believe in God."

"Why did he move here?"

"While overseas working for God, his wife was murdered. He returned to the States broken hearted... Still believes in God, though. He ended up coming down here to do some kind of home missionary work. Guess he figured that folks here needed religion."

* * *

Larry, Quinn, and Mary Jo ran as fast as they could, the sound of barking and howling dogs fading behind them. When they reached the stream that Ethel had told them about, Larry sprinkled pepper around and behind them. Then they crossed the shallow part of the stream to the other side. As they ran, one of them occasionally tripped and fell to the ground. They ran for several hundred yards until Larry called a halt.

"Give me your belt, your shoelaces, and your necklace, too," he told the girl.

He scavenged for additional items in the woods, and when he returned, he and Mary Jo worked together to build a very clever trap. Quinn watched them and wondered how two people from such different backgrounds could possibly be on the same wavelength.

Noticing her attention, a pleased looking Mary Jo said, "We're playmates."

"I can tell," Quinn responded, and for some reason, the thought gave her a chill. Was the girl mentally challenged? Her intellect sometimes seemed like that of a child, and she wasn't comfortable with the bond the girl seemed to be forming with Larry.

Larry tossed the remaining pepper around and threw the can aside before stepping into the water up to his knees.

* * *

In the mountain gulch, the Mayor and his posse heard a commotion in the weeds nearby and cornered Larry's scent. They drew their guns and, with itchy trigger fingers, moved cautiously forward.

"We got ya now, city slicker," Butch gleefully shouted. "Come out with yer hands up."

But when they pulled back the weeds, all they found was Old Ethel's dog with Larry's shirt tied around her neck.

"Damn her," the Mayor growled. "Once I get my hands on those kids, I'm going back to take care of that old bat. Split into two groups and backtrack."

Chapter Thirteen

"Let's go," Larry said.

Quinn followed, but Mary Jo stopped when the water reached her ankles.

"I never go that far," she said.

"It's okay!" Larry assured her. "It's shallow."

"Let's move," Quinn urged. "Quickly, or they'll catch us."

"I don't want to be locked up again," Mary Jo said.

"Then we need to get out of here," Quinn said.

Mary Jo's face was etched with fear and uncertainty. She cautiously moved forward, more uncomfortable with every step until she tripped on a stone under the water. She screamed, and when Larry caught her, she scratched at him and pounded his arms with her fist as she tried to flee.

"What the hell are you doing?" Larry complained. "Ow! Hey! I'm your friend. I'm on your side. It's okay. You're safe. We're playmates, remember?"

He gently grabbed her arms, and she calmed down as he held her in a gentle hug. Quinn eyed him, her expression questioning and suspicious. To her way of thinking, Larry was getting just a little too friendly with Mary Jo.

The lady in question looked into his eyes, her expression innocently trusting. "You're my playmate?" She asked.

"Sure, but we have to be quiet," Larry warned, placing a finger to her lips. "So that the bad men don't find us."

He took her hand, and together, they stepped out further into the stream. But after taking a couple of steps, the sandy bottom dropped over a foot, and the current grew stronger. Pulling them away from the shallow water and into the deeper water that lay ahead. Mary Jo screamed and fell into Larry's ready grasp. Quinn lunged for them, but the current was too strong, and all three were helplessly pulled downstream.

Further away in the woods, the group of men heard Mary Jo's scream and stopped, hushing their dogs and listening.

"This way," the Mayor shouted. "That was Mary Jo. I'd recognize her scream anywhere. Get them!"

As Quinn, Larry, and Mary Jo fought the current, they took turns grabbing onto each other as the current tossed them about like fishing bobbers.

"Larry!" Quinn shouted as she desperately tried to swim toward shore.

"Quinn!" Larry called. "Don't fight the current. Let it carry you downstream. It's the quickest way to put some distance between them and us."

Mary Jo continued screaming, and she began flailing in the water and scratching Larry once more.

As the posse rushed toward the area, Hank and Harrison led the way, searching the path with the dogs in front. Within moments, they reached the traps that Larry and Mary Jo had set. Fortunately, the dogs easily avoided them, but when Hank stepped forward, he released the first trap, a thick branch that whipped out and struck him in the face, causing him to fall backward and hit the ground.

Harrison burst out laughing. "Woo wee, Hank got suckered by a Yankee!"

His laughter was cut short when another branch immediately whipped out, striking him in the same way. He dropped to the ground next to Hank. Both men were knocked out and had bloody noses. The Mayor shook his head in wonder.

"That city kid sure is good."

* * *

Having had no luck finding the three fugitives, Packy and Jamal headed back to the Sheriff's office. The Sheriff poured himself another cup of coffee and sat behind his desk, but Jamal was restless. If he'd had his way, they would still be out looking. Especially after they had found all the vehicles, which had been at Shaky Pete's, parked at the Mayor's house. Packy had not wanted to take Jamal any further, saying that his life would be in danger, too, if they ran into that crowd. Unable to settle down and relax, Jamal gravitated over to the wall with the missing girls' photos. Although he knew such horror existed, he couldn't come to terms with the fact that these girls were all dead. He examined their photos:

One had blonde hair and was wearing a blue blouse and tight-fitting jeans.

Another had auburn hair and a beautiful smile. She wore a peach top and a white mini skirt.

The third had brown hair cut short and was wearing a navy blue running suit and jogging shoes.

He marveled at the length of the next one's hair, which appeared to go all the way down to the top of her thighs. She wore a red blouse, jean skirt, and a pair of red shoes… One of which he had found at the Mayor's house that now rested in his pocket. If he hadn't been convinced before, he was now. Jamal was certain that he knew the identity of the killer. Trouble was he was pretty sure the Sheriff did, too. What mystified him was the fact that Packy either didn't want to believe it or was, for some reason, protecting him.

"I'd be surprised if your friends are still alive," Packy said. "That was an ugly crowd tonight if they're anything like the men back at Pete's. I hate to say it, but if I hadn't found you when I did, they might have drowned you in that toilet." He turned and noticed the young man looking at the photos. "You shouldn't look at those. It's too depressing."

"I've been studying photos a lot lately. Quinn is quite good with a camera. She seems to be able to capture a person's essence with every shot she takes. Whoever took these photos knew these girls intimately, or at the very least wanted to."

"What makes you say that?" Packy asked, surprised.

"Their soul and story are in each picture."

His words took Packy by surprise and sent his mind back to the latest crime scene and his deputy, who had almost gleefully photographed the body. Now that he thought about it, it did seem like Dale was taking a little too much pleasure as he took those photographs.

* * *

Things went from bad to worse as the trio was pulled along the rain-swollen creek. Fifty feet from where they had lost their balance, Larry spotted a large tree branch hanging out over the water. He managed to grab hold of it and was finally able to drag the three of them to the other side of the stream. Larry, Quinn, and Mary Joe walked up the bank, shivering from the icy cold water. Larry and Quinn lay back on the grass and caught their breath.

"It's okay," Larry said to Mary Jo, who remained standing and looking fearfully around. "It's okay. Come on! We're gonna get help."

But it seemed that Mary Jo no longer wanted to play along. "I wanna go home," she said, almost pitifully.

"I know," Larry assured her. "So do I. We'll get you there eventually. Where do you live anyways?"

Mary Jo did not answer. Instead, she shivered and sat beside him. He sat up and wrapped his arms around her to warm her. Quinn stood up and watched the cuddling pair, wondering about Larry's actions toward the strange girl. In the shadows and unbeknownst to them, two eyes watched the three of them.

"You okay?" He asked Quinn.

She nodded. "It seems you're pretty good yourself. You were supposed to be saving her, not jumping her. And in the river, that looked more like groping than it did grabbing."

The bushes rustled, but they were too wrapped up in their own conversation and didn't notice.

"I was grabbing her so that she wouldn't go downstream without us," Larry objected, "just like I did with you."

"Yeah, when we were dating, you used to grab me, just like that," Quinn replied sarcastically.

Suddenly, a wild boar shot out of the bushes and charged them. It wasn't the mother sow that had attacked them before. Larry tackled Quinn, saving her from serious injury. Mary Jo picked up a fair-sized rock and threw it at the boar. At ran off squealing.

Larry did not release Quinn immediately, turning his embrace into a close intimate moment.

"This is not the time," Quinn said, disgusted. She gave him a nasty look and pulled away.

Once they scrambled up, Mary Jo joined them. Grinning, Larry led the way through the damp forest. He was about to make a snide remark when a raccoon trap caught his foot with a mighty snap.

"Argh!" Larry cried out as he fell writhing to the ground.

Quinn and Mary Jo knelt down, and together they worked to open the trap and release his foot.

"Thanks," Larry said, once the trap was finally removed. "I think my foot is bruised but not broken, thanks to my heavy shoes."

Quinn helped him to his feet, causing more pain to shoot through his injured foot and up his leg. Wincing in sympathy, Quinn and Mary Jo supported him as they moved on.

Still, in pursuit, the Mayor and his men looked everywhere. With no more screams to guide them, the dogs were once more sniffing for the trail, but when they reached the riverbank, the animals began sneezing and looking confused. Clearly, they had lost the trail.

"What's happening?" Hank asked.

The Mayor became suspicious, and bending down, he picked up the empty tin can Larry had tossed aside and examined it. The label said black pepper.

"It's pepper," the Mayor said in disgust. "That old hag gave them a can of pepper." He slammed the can down on the ground and crushed it with his foot. "Split up! Go! Go! Go! Come on! I want them city slickers found."

After walking for another thirty minutes, the three fugitives came to an old mine shaft. The entrance was paved with coal rock. They were surprised when they spotted a well-fueled fire burning in a steel drum several feet inside the mine's entrance. Larry, Quinn, and Mary Jo eyed their surroundings. No one appeared to be around, and the women shivered. Larry placed his arms around both of them as they huddled over the hot flames. The orange glow from the fire brought rosy warmth to their cheeks and began to dry their damp clothes.

"Perfect!" Quinn said. "The mountains can sure get cold at night. Even in the summer. Brrrr."

Two eyes in the shadows appeared and watched. They were the same eyes that had watched them before. Turning to Mary Jo, Larry decided to try once more to find out the girl's name.

"I'm Larry. This is Quinn. Who are you?"

"Mary Jo," she said after a long pause.

The dogs' barking became audible again, agitating Mary Jo.

"I'm really sorry for all that's happened to you," Quinn said when she saw the fear return to the girl's face. "It'll all be over soon. Let's get going."

They stepped away from the fire to head toward town when suddenly, the wooden floorboards gave out, and the three companions fell down an air shaft, rolling and tumbling until first Quinn and then Larry grabbed a long thick root to halt their fall. Larry snatched Mary Jo's hand as she shot past him, and when he pulled her up, she, too, grabbed hold of the root. Then the old toothless bum came out of hiding, leaned over the ledge, and gave them a toothless smile.

"You okay? Wanna shot? Best moonshine in the county!"

Even though they were too far down to reach it, he extended a flask.

"Forget the moonshine," Larry shouted. He was clearly exasperated. "Get us out of here!"

"You got money?"

"What?" Larry couldn't believe his ears.

"You got money?" The toothless bum insisted.

They slipped further, causing coal dust to fall all around them. Mary Jo clawed at Larry and kicked her legs, trying to find a place to brace herself.

"Stop it!" Larry growled at Mary Jo. Looking up at the bum, he said, "You've got to be kidding!"

The bum extended his hand and wiggled his fingers, clearly insisting on being paid before giving them any help.

"Fine," Larry capitulated. "If I have to pay you to help aside here, I'll do it."

"I already *gave* you money earlier," Quinn shouted.

The bum cocked his head and thought. "That's right. You did, didn't ya?"

He disappeared. Thinking they had been abandoned, Quinn was about to beg him to come back when a rope dropped down. Quinn pulled herself up and quickly disappeared. Larry grabbed the rope and tried to pull Mary Jo above him to go next, but she resisted his help.

"Hey, pull up the rope!" He told the bum.

Having heard footsteps outside the mine entrance, the toothless bum once more disappeared. The Mayor crept up to the mine and suspiciously shined the light inside.

"I know you're in there. Yer cornered! You can't survive. Come on out, and I promise you won't get hurt."

Quinn moved out of sight, stepping back further in the mine and pressed her body against the wall in the darkness. Then, the bum eerily stepped out of the shadows, catching the Mayor off guard.

"They ain't in there!" He said as he stepped closer to the Mayor.

The Mayor took a step inside and peered around him. "Where are they then?"

"How much money you got?"

In the airshaft, Larry could barely see or hear the two men above. The Mayor stood close to the hole and looked down. He didn't see anyone, and as he stepped away to avoid falling down the shaft, his shoes nudged some of the gravel, causing it to fall into the hole. It stung as it hit his and Mary Jo's faces, and they inched down the root a little further. Holding on with one hand, Larry used the other to cover the girl's mouth as she tugged and pulled. Hearing the noise, the Mayor shined the light into the air shaft. If they hadn't moved, they would have been spotted. As it was, the beam narrowly missed them.

Above, the bum extended his flask in front of the Mayor's face. Irritated, the politician brushed it aside.

"You got money? I'll tell ya where they be," the bum offered with a grin.

The Mayor raised his crossbow and pointed it at the bum's heart.

"Ha! Give me yer money. Everything!" The bum crowd seemingly oblivious to the threat the weapon posed.

Sighing in disgust, the Mayor reached into his pocket and handed over a wad of small bills. The bum stuffed them into the front pocket of his pants. He hesitated a moment before pointing down the trail away from the mine.

"They went that away."

The Mayor and his posse hurried away, and Quinn came out from hiding. Larry desperately held on as he strained to hear the old man's response. He heard nothing but silence until, suddenly, the rope once more dropped down, and the man's face appeared.

"Grab it. He's gone! Got yer money?"

Quinn was tempted to grab the rope away from the old man and push them away, but she was afraid she wouldn't be strong enough to haul both Larry and Mary Jo to the surface. Grabbing the rope, Larry and Mary Jo climbed upward until they could pull themselves out of the shaft. They emerged covered in coal dust.

"My money," the bum said. "Give me my money."

Larry dug into his wallet and pulled out some bills, making sure he kept the hundred dollar bill, he had flashed around earlier, hidden from sight.

"I'll take that shot now," he told the old man.

The bum handed over the flask as Quinn and Mary Jo headed for the fire barrel to warm themselves. Larry took a healthy drink and coughed. As he did, the bum noticed Mary Jo's face through the flames and moved closer for a better look.

"Hey! I know you."

Larry turned just in time to see the old man grab a nail ridden board, and race toward her swinging his weapon and shouting, "I'm going to save you!"

Chapter Fourteen

Mary Jo held up her hands in self-defense as Larry grabbed hold of the other end of the board and tried to wrestle it from the bum's hands. The old man tried to kick him, and when he didn't have much luck with that, he punched him in the gut. Larry doubled over, gasping for air. In the commotion, Mary Jo was knocked to the ground. She tried to scoot away on her hands and feet, but the bum grabbed her ankle, laughing and panting as he got a better grip on the board.

"You got the devil in you, missy… But don't you worry… I'll beat him out, so he never troubles you again."

As he raised his weapon, ready to strike. And she covered her head and screamed. But before the board could hit her, Larry punched the bum in the nose with a meaty fist, knocking him to the ground. The old man grabbed Larry's bad ankle and tripped him, then he squirmed away. Mary Jo screamed in fright, Larry screamed in pain. Quinn ran to them both, and after pulling Larry to his feet, the three of them quickly ran away. Having seen which direction the Mayor and his party had taken, Quinn steered them in the opposite direction.

"Stop!" The bum shouted. "You can't get the devil out of her. You don't know how. She'll get you before you even try. You hear me?"

Fortunately for Mary Jo, Larry and Quinn ignored the old man's words and kept running.

* * *

Sometime later, the Mayor stood in his front yard, waving goodbye to the good ole boys, with a weak smile plastered on his face. They hadn't found Mary Jo and the

149

out-of-towners, and this worried him plenty. For now, all he could do was hope that the three of them would find their way to the Sheriff's office, where Packy would take care of things.

"Thanks, boys," the Mayor called. "Thanks for coming out."

Everyone drove off.

* * *

Back at the sheriff's station, the drunk and Jamal sat in a cell, playing a game of gin rummy. Larry, Quinn, and Mary Jo breathlessly burst in the front door.

"Sheriff," Larry called. "I've got her, Sheriff!"

They spotted Jamal in the cell with another man.

Jamal jumped to his feet. "Get out! Run! You've got to get out of here!"

"What the hell are you doing in there?" Larry asked.

"The Sheriff and the Mayor are in it together," Jamal replied.

"Where are the keys?" Larry said as he searched through the office. He tried not to panic as he wondered how they would keep the girl sane and get out of town with their lives.

"Somewhere on the desk," the drunken man told him.

Larry rummaged through the drawers and its contents. When he finally found them, he hurried to the cell door and frantically fumbled through the different keys, trying each one to see if it was the right key. Outside, a car door slammed just as Larry unlocked the cell. They ran for the door, but as Larry jerked it open, the Sheriff entered with his shotgun pointed at the young man's chest.

"Don't move," Packy ordered. "No more running."

150

The Mayor came through the back door a moment later and stood beside the Sheriff.

"Well, well, well. Here we are again, one big happy family. You youngins have been poking your noses where they don't belong. I'd say it's time to take care of that."

Larry's eyes shifted toward Quinn, who nodded in silent understanding. She cued Jamal, who sighed, but stood ready.

"Go, go, go!" Larry shouted.

The three friends charged the Sheriff and Mayor, knocking them off balance, but not for long. Raising his gun, Packy fired into the ceiling, knocking some of the plaster to the floor.

"Quinn, go!" Larry urged.

Quinn grabbed Mary Jo by the hand and pulled her out the door.

"Are you my new playmate?" Mary Jo asked as they flew down the street and ducked between one of the boarded-up buildings in the alley next to Shaky Pete's.

They darted around mounds of trash and several empty beer crates, straining to see in the darkness. Then to make things worse, Mary Jo started struggling, trying to pull her hand out of Quinn's as she searched for a good hiding place.

"Come on!" Quinn whispered fiercely as she fought to hang on to the girl's hand. She was puzzled over Mary Jo's rapid personality changes and wondered, not for the first time if she was mentally handicapped. "Don't you understand? They're going to kill you! Let's go!"

"Kill…kill?" Mary Jo muttered mournfully. "I'm sorry."

Mary Jo kept turning and looking back at the jailhouse, and she didn't see a particularly large mound of trash until it was too late. She toppled over it and hit the ground.

Quinn felt sorry for her companion. Maybe she really didn't understand what was going on and that her life was in jeopardy. "Careful," she said gently. "Don't hurt yourself."

As Quinn helped her up, Mary Jo freed her hand and grabbed a sharp, pointed, scrap metal bar that was sticking out of the trash next to where she fell. Quinn didn't notice.

"I want to go home!" Mary Jo insisted as she got a better grip on the weapon and prepared to strike.

Back at the jail, Jamal and Larry fought with Packy and the Mayor, trading punches and dodging blows in order to buy Quinn and Mary Jo more time. Packy shoved Larry against the wall of his office and stepped back from the fight.

"Stop!" Packy shouted. "You don't understand!"

Neither Larry nor Jamal listened. Jamal punched the Mayor in the face as Larry engaged the Sheriff once more and fought for possession of the shotgun. They struggled for control until Larry wrested the weapon from Packy's grip. As he did, the gun fired, bringing all four men to a halt as they looked around to see if anyone was hurt.

"That's enough!" Larry shouted as he pointed the gun at Packy and the Mayor. "Everybody stop! I'm calling the shots, now!"

Exhausted and not wanting to risk being shot, the Mayor and the Sheriff raised their hands in the air and surrendered.

The Sheriff sighed and laughed a bit shakily. "You don't understand…," he insisted.

"Shut up! I'm the one with the gun, now," Larry demanded.

The Mayor chuckled and wiped the blood away from his mouth.

"What's so funny, fatty?" Jamal growled.

"You city folks… always thinking you have everything figured out. You look at people, and because you believe you're better than us simple folk, you think you know everything there is to know. But you don't have any idea about what's going on."

"What are you talking about?" Larry demanded.

"That girl that you're so hell-bent on rescuing… She's our sister, Mary Jo," the Mayor told them.

Larry and Jamal exchanged amazed glances.

"Sister?" Larry asked.

"You're kidding… Right?" Jamal insisted.

Packy sadly shook his head. "She's violently crazy. Mary Jo attacks people when she gets nervous, sorta short-circuits, and then starts hurting folks. That's what you saw from the train. We have to keep her locked up for her own protection."

Larry's hand flew up to his cheek, and he felt the scratches she had left there.

"That's why she came after me with that knife," the Mayor explained.

"That's what you saw through the window of the train," Sheriff Packy added. "She had snuck out of the house and was attackin' Patrick, who was doing nothing more than tryin' to catch and keep her from runnin' away and getting' hurt or hurting someone else."

"That's right. You see, Mary Jo was taken away from us after our mother died," the Mayor explained. "The county put her up in a dungeon of a mental hospital that was more like a prison than a medical facility. We tried everything we could think of to find help for her, but we were unable to get her the proper treatment. And she was so miserable at that place that we wanted to get her out of there."

"And we couldn't stand the abusiveness the patients suffered from several of the personnel. It was so bad that the state finally closed down the facility, and we brought her home," Packy said. "There just wasn't any place else to put her that seemed any better than the last one. So we decided to care for her at home."

* * *

As he finished speaking, Packy's mind flashed back to the time when Mary Jo had been incarcerated in that awful place. The mental hospital had dirty linoleum flooring, and the patients' beds were unmade unless the patient made it, showing gray, discolored linens that didn't see a washing machine nearly as often as they should have. Although the orderlies were more careful whenever visitors were around, they usually made fun of the mentally ill, showed little patience or compassion toward them, and often used greater physical force than was required. Packy also suspected that some of the doctors and nurses had been performing cruel and unnecessary experiments on the patients.

* * *

Packy's mind returned to the present. "Bobby walled off part of the attic and made it really nice for her to stay in. The enclosed space makes her feel safe, and she actually prefers to stay there most of the time," he said.

Larry and Jamal exchanged glances. There he felt like an idiot. It would seem that all this had been for nothing.

"She's not kidnapped?" Larry asked.

"Nope," the Mayor confirmed, shaking his head. "We were trying to protect you from her. Frankly, I'm surprised you're alive, but now your friend is alone with her, and she is in grave danger."

Suddenly, Jamal felt something stinging his backside and fainted. Apparently, the Mayor had shot him with his crossbow, but in all the excitement, Jamal didn't feel the pain until after everything calmed down.

"Pat, why don't you take this boy to the hospital?" He turned to Larry. "You wanna help me save your girlfriend?"

"She's not my girlfriend," Larry said. "At least, not anymore."

In the alley behind Shaky Pete's, the two girls hid behind a tall stack of empty beer crates. Peeking around it gave them a partial view of the Sheriff's office. As the sky brightened, Quinn watched intently, waiting to see who would come through the door.

"I don't see anyone," she said after twenty minutes. "Come on. We're gonna go get help."

Mary Jo didn't say a word, but Quinn didn't think anything of it until an odd noise made her spin around to find the wrath-filled girl coming right at her with the sharp metal bar.

"Playmate!" Mary Jo yelled. Her eyes gleamed with insanity.

Quinn screamed in reaction and fell back, deflecting the attack, but Mary Jo jumped on top of her, and the two women wrestled for control of the weapon as Mary Jo repeatedly stabbed at Quinn.

"I'm sorry. I'm sorry. I'm sorry," Mary Jo wailed mournfully as she continued attacking Quinn. "Please forgive me, but playmate must pay."

"Help me!" Quinn screamed. "*Stop!*"

Quinn fought hard, but Mary Jo grabbed her by the hair and smashed her head against the ground. Dazed, Quinn lay there helpless as Mary Jo raised the metal bar high to kill her. As the weapon began the downward stroke of what would be a fatal blow, the Sheriff tackled Mary Jo and firmly but carefully held her down. The girl grunted and roared with frustration as she tried to break free of his grip.

"It's okay now, Mary Jo," Packy soothed her. "It's okay, honey. Hush now."

Larry rushed over to Quinn and helped her up. She hugged him fiercely, relieved that, at last, this nightmare might finally be over.

The Sheriff lovingly brushed his sister's hair from her face as he spoke to her in a quiet voice. "It's okay, Mary Jo. Brother is here. Shh, it's okay. Nobody meant anything bad. I've come to take you home."

Chapter Fifteen

Warm rays of light emerged over the tall pine trees of the Appellation Mountains. As the sun broke over the horizon, it painted the sky over the sleepy Dobson Valley orange and pink. As color returned to the landscape, the dark shadows receded, but not for everyone.

Katie lay on the bare floor, a moaning whimper escaping her lips. "Help me. Please, someone…please let me go."

An uncaring eye watched through a hole.

* * *

As the town awoke to a new day, Larry, Jamal, and Quinn sat around a metal table in the diner a few doors down from Shaky Pete's with the Mayor, Sheriff Packy, and their sister, Mary Jo. Three men passed them as they headed for a table in the corner.

"After mom took ill, I tried to take care of Mary Jo," Patrick explained. "But the state didn't think we could provide the kind of care she needed. They took her away and placed her in a cold, dirty mental institution."

"I visited every week for a year, but she was so unhappy," Packy said. "I figured that we'd had a stroke of good fortune when the state closed down the mental hospital and turned the patients away. Pat took her in."

"She becomes agitated whenever she's in an open space for very long. And certain sounds and colors can set her off quicker than anything. So I built a false wall in the attic," the Mayor said. "And she got so attached to that room that she didn't want to be in any other. She's a handful, but it works out for the best."

Everyone smiled as Mary Jo lovingly leaned against her brother, Patrick's shoulder. A moment later, Tommy Wallace and Darlene Tucker, wearing the clothes she had worn the previous night along with a wedding veil, barged into the bar.

"Hi, everyone, guess what? I'm married!" Darlene happily announced.

"Orange juice for everyone, I'm buying!" Tommy shouted.

The early morning crowd applauded, and Darlene tossed her bouquet. It landed in Harrison's lap. The three friends smiled, thinking all was well.

"Patrick's been the better brother," Sheriff Packy admitted. "Except for official business, I really haven't seen much of him over the last two years. We've lived in two different worlds most of our life. That has to change. I'm really sorry that Mary Jo got so violent last night."

"It's okay," Quinn replied. "You got there just in time, so no harm done."

Mary Jo looked a bit ashamed, but smiled, nonetheless. She beamed and hugged Patrickagain. She seemed so peaceful…so beautiful that Larry smiled, grateful that everything had worked out.

Two couples, who had passed their table earlier, finished eating and paid their checks just as several of the men, who had been in the bar last night, entered the diner. They were all cleaned up and hardly recognizable. Jake had his little girl with him. The Sheriff studied Clyde, who was wearing a fresh pair of muddy boots that left a trail of dirt as he walked across the tiled floor.

"Sorry about last night," Wilson said. "We thought you'd kidnapped Mary Jo."

"Really… sorry," Jake added.

"That's okay," Jamal said. "Don't worry about it."

"Was Clyde with you boys last night?" The Sheriff asked.

"No," Leonard replied. "He said he had things to do and had to stay home."

"I think I'd best be getting Mary Jo home," the Mayor said. "It been a night full of close calls, and we're all beat."

"I'll give you a ride to the train station," Packy told Larry and his friends. "The train should be arriving soon."

As they exited the diner, Shaky Pete ran into them. He secretly handed Larry a brown bag with a bottle of moonshine inside and winked. "You left this at the bar."

As Pete slipped away, Larry opened the bag and realizing it contained moonshine, grinned. A short while later, the three friends and the Sheriff arrived at the train station.

Larry walked to the ticket window and pulled out his deck of credit cards, but he hesitated. Turning away from the clerk and looking at his friends, he said, "Uh…"

"What's wrong," Quinn asked.

"I need help," he admitted. "I don't have enough money for the fare, and my credit cards are maxed out."

Jamal stepped up to the window and paid for their tickets from a big wad of cash he had earned as tips. Turning to Larry, he said, "You can put the credit cards away."

"Thanks." Larry's reply was heartfelt as he stuffed the cards into his pocket, and he felt a huge weight lift from his shoulders. He was amazed at how good he felt, now that he was no longer pretending to be rich and worldly.

Packy helped them pull their bags out of the storage closet.

"I was wrong about you and your friends," he told Larry. "You aren't so bad for Yankees."

"And I was wrong about you and yours," Larry admitted. "Not a bad town you have here. Maybe on the way back, we'll stop by and say hello."

"I'd like that," Packy said. "Believe it or not, we *do* have more interesting places to visit than the bar."

Everyone laughed as the train whistled and pulled into the station. When the door to the boarding car opened, Jamal breathed a sigh of relief. "Whew! I'm so glad to see this train. I could kiss it."

Quinn smiled at him and then gave the sheriff a hug before turning to leave. After tugging on Larry's sleeve, she boarded the train, but Larry turned back to the Sheriff.

"What about your sister?" Larry asked him. "You gonna hide her up there forever?"

"No. After this, I realize that Mary Jo needs the right kind of care. I'll find the money to place her somewhere they can help her," the Sheriff replied.

"Here's the red shoe we found at the Mayor's house," Jamal said as he handed it to the Sheriff. "I meant to give this back to you earlier." Turning, he boarded the train.

"Thanks. I'll see that she gets it," Packy replied. "Here's my card. Give me a call the next time you're in the area."

Larry put the card in his wallet.

"You know, it's all Quinn's fault for spotting Mary Jo's shoe under the dresser and taking a photo," Larry said jokingly. "Otherwise, we never would have gone back. I hope you catch your killer."

"I'm thinking of forming a task force," Packy said. "Things have gotten so far out of hand that I now realize I can't do this alone. You take care."

"You, too," Larry replied. "Good hunting."

The two waved, and Larry boarded the train. Packy returned to his Jeep and headed into town.

At the home of Deputy Clark, Dale could hear a faint moaning coming from one of the upper rooms in his home, and he moved up the stairs.

Tired from the long, event-filled night, Packy drove straight home. Entering his house, he dropped his keys on the table next to the door, moved into the bedroom, and flopped down on his bed. Rolling onto his back, he stared at the ceiling and smiled, relieved that this awful night was finally over. Closing his heavy eyelids, he yawned. Then his eyes flew open in alarm as Larry's words come back to him, filling him with dread like a bell tolling for the dead.

You know, it's all Quinn's fault for seeing Mary Jo's shoe under the dresser and taking a photo.

Packy bolted upright, realizing something that sent a shiver down his spine.

* * *

On the train, Jamal placed his baggage in the overhead compartment and dropped into the aisle seat. Larry sat next to him by the window, taking a breather. A few seats away, an elderly woman struggled to lift her suitcase and shove it onto the overhead rack. Quinn, who sat across the aisle from the guys, raised her camera to take a picture, but after a moment's thought, she stopped. Setting the camera aside, she hurried over to the woman and helped, receiving a warm smile in return that gave her a wonderful feeling inside, which surprised her.

Moments later, the Amtrak slowly pulled out of the station after allowing an oncoming passenger train to pass.

* * *

Deputy Clark moved closer and closer to the bed, where a whimpering form in a white nightgown watched him approach. When he reached her, his sickly mother looked upon him with loving eyes. He smiled as he sat on the bed next to her and patted her hand.

"How ya feeling, Momma?"

She touched her son's face. "Much better now that you're here. You're such a good boy."

He reached down and tenderly kissed her cheek.

* * *

After delivering the moonshine to Larry, Pete returned to his bar and slipped through the back door. Looking around to make sure that no one was watching, he quickly opened the door to his shed and went inside. A complex machine of tubes, boiler, and barrels chugged away. Pete hurried over to his moaning still and began bottling a new batch of moonshine.

* * *

On the train, Larry closed his eyes and rested his head against the window, hoping he would sleep for the rest of the journey. As he did, his mind drifted back to the series of events that had led to their recent adventure, reliving the moment when the frightened girl had banged on the train window. Her face no longer a blur, he mentally concentrated on her features and the blood on her hands, but for some reason, the image he saw was not

Mary Joe. Then his mind focused on the close-up image of the tattoo on the girl's wrist, and he forced himself to picture the girl he thought he was saving from a serial killer.

Like a camera focusing on a close-up, his mind flashed again, and he saw Mary Jo's wrist in the woods as she struggled with him. There was no tattoo there, only cuts made from several attempted suicides. As the scene played out in his mind, he thought. *Wasn't it odd how Mary Jo kept talking about her 'playmate?'* Nevertheless, the realization still hadn't sunk in.

"You know," he said, addressing his friends, "the thing I can't quite wrap my head around in all of this is: if Mary Jo wasn't in any real danger…then that means there's still a serial killer murdering girls in Dobson Valley."

"I was just thinking the same thing. But something puzzles me," Jamal agreed. "I had a chance to study the missing girl's photos in the Sheriff's office. One of the victims was wearing a red shoe that, I believe, matched the one we found at the Mayor's house exactly."

Jamal's words hit Larry like a steam engine running full-speed at the blocked tunnel. Energized, he stood up and looked out the window at the moving countryside. A second later, he stepped over his friend's legs and ran for the conductor.

* * *

Having gone back to his office, Packy stood looking at the picture of the missing girl, wearing one red shoe. Pulling out the shoe Jamal had given him, he compared it to the photograph. And it hit him. They were exactly the same.

"No! It can't be…"

He bolted out of the office just as Larry began explaining his urgent need to use a landline to call the Sheriff's office. The conductor listened patiently.

Driving as fast as he dared, Packy raced to the Mayor's house. He did not use his lights or siren as he didn't want his brother to know he was coming. Upon arrival, he left his vehicle and hurried up the porch steps. Then he carefully turned the knob, and the door creaked open. After drawing his gun, Packy poked his head in.

"Patrick?" He gently called out.

Nothing happened. So he quietly entered the house. He heard humming coming from the kitchen and soundlessly moved to the doorway and peeked around the corner. Mary Jo sang to herself as she washed and dried the dishes from the previous night. Not wishing to alert her to his presence, he moved toward the staircase and slid along the wall as he headed upstairs, his gun pointing the way.

Packy checked each bedroom as he passed, but he found no one inside, so he went up the next flight of steps and entered the attic, carefully looking around. The stairs came up in the center of the attic, and as he walked across the floor, it creaked. Counting his steps to each wall, he discovered that it was twelve feet in one direction and eight feet in the other, which was odd. He knew the attic would be a lot bigger than that. Then he remembered his brother saying that he had walled off part of the space. On the wall eight feet from the center, Packy saw that boxes had been moved up against it. He pulled them away and found a stool in front of a small round hole in the wall. *That's odd.* Why would his brother have placed a peephole there?

He looked through the hole and saw Katie bound, gagged, and crying, strapped to a chair that had been nailed to the floor. An untouched plate of crusty food sat near her feet, and a number of dolls surrounded the chair, all of them dismembered. Packy quickly found the door and entered into the hidden section of the attic.

"Dear God…"

As soon as the Sheriff entered the room, Katie screamed through her gag.

"Calm down. I'm here to rescue you," Packy told her. "Everything is going to be okay."

He hurriedly untied her and removed the gag from her mouth.

"Please! You have to get me out of here!" Katie wailed. "I want to go home. I don't want to die!"

"Shh, it's gonna be okay," the Sheriff reassured her. "I've got ya."

As he spoke, he heard footsteps coming up the staircase. Leading Katie to the attic window, he helped her get safely out. Katie slid down onto the porch roof, and from there, grabbed the spouting, sliding down it until she reached the ground. The Sheriff watched her run across the backyard and head for home. He briefed a sigh of relief. Hearing someone behind him, he tensed but did not turn around.

"Mary Jo's feet are small, and she doesn't own a pair of red shoes," Packy said quietly. Turning, he found the Mayor aiming a crossbow at him. "Patrick, what the hell is this? This is sick!"

"How would you know?" Patrick asked. "You were never around. I was the one who took care of mom when we were young. I was the one who took care of Mary Jo the past two years. And neither was happy or satisfied with what I did for them."

Wondering why his brother was pointing a weapon at him, an expression of disbelief suddenly crossed Packy's face.

"Pat, God no, not you," he accused him in a shocked voice. "You killed all those girls… It was you this whole time. That's how you sidetracked me from all those clues. You used our relationship to divert me." He paused a moment before continuing. "I'm sorry, but I'm going to have to place you under arrest."

Packy pulled a pair of handcuffs out of his back pocket.

"No," the Mayor replied, shocked. "You don't believe *I* killed the girls, do you? It wasn't me, Packy." His voice shook when he continued. "It was our sister. She killed them."

"Mary Jo? No. What are you saying?"

"She demanded that I bring her a playmate," Patrick said. "When she killed the first one, I thought it was an accident. It wasn't until the second death that I realized that she was really crazy, just like mom had been. But I couldn't report her. I couldn't send her back to some cold, dark place or worse yet to prison."

The brothers stared at each other in despair.

"I'm going to have to bring the two of you in for kidnapping and murder, Patrick. You know that, don't you?"

"I can't let you do that, Packy. Who will look after our mother?"

"What?" Packy asked, confused.

The Sheriff walked toward his brother, but when Patrick took a step backward, he fell, accidentally firing the crossbow and hitting Packy in the chest. The Sheriff cried out in pain. Clutching the wound, he looked down at the bow, over at his brother, and then up at his sister, who was now standing behind the fallen Mayor. His eyes were filled with shock and pain as they rolled up in his head, and he dropped to the floor, never to rise again.

Chapter Sixteen

The Mayor looked up from his position on the floor at his sister, who, although she had her father's eyes and chin, still looked so much like their mother. His mind flashed back to when he was twelve-years-old.

* * *

Standing in a shed with his mother and siblings, he trembled in front of a dead deer. Their mother appeared half crazy. In the corner of the shed stood his four-year-old brother, Packy, holding his two-year-old sister, Mary Jo's hand.

"Now skin it, Pat. I did the hard part of killing it," his mother said. "Go ahead. It's dead. It isn't anything but meat now, and it'll feed us for months to come."

Patrick glanced up at his mother, his mouth partially open. He was breathing hard as he returned his gaze to the deer. He swallowed convulsively, incapable of moving or taking the skinning knife she held out to him.

"You can't do anything right, can you?" his mother said in disgust. "You're a bad, bad boy."

* * *

Patrick's memory melted away, and his eyes refocused to find Mary Jo still standing over him. As he looked up at her, what he thought was his mother's face swirled and changed, becoming Mary Jo.

"You are so bad," Mary Jo scolded, looking down at him. Her voice was nothing like their mother's. "You really are a bad boy. You can't do anything right."

"I tried to make you happy," the Mayor whined.

Mary Jo lowered the shotgun she was carrying. She shook with rage as the shell exploded from the muzzle.

* * *

The silver Amtrak train idled at the next station, waiting for its passenger to return. Larry stood in a telephone booth a few feet away. The conductor stood behind him. He would have used his cell phone from the train, but there was no signal this deep in the mountains. Fortunately, he had the Sheriff's card in his pocket, so he had the number of the station.

The phone was answered on the second ring by the deputy.

"Sheriff's office."

"Deputy Clark, there's another girl at the Mayor's house," Larry warned.

"I know, Larry. Katie escaped and is home safe and sound, but the Mayor and the Sheriff are both dead. They killed each other. I have no idea where Mary Jo is. She must be scared out of her mind and lost in the woods. We've got everyone out searching the forest for her, but don't worry, we'll find her."

Larry was shocked and saddened to hear about Packy's death. "I'm sorry about the Sheriff. I was looking forward to getting to know him better. I hope you find Mary Jo before she kills anyone else. I guess we shall have to go to prison now."

"I don't know," Dale said. "Once we find her, we'll have a town meeting to see if we can work something out. She really belongs in an institution, not a prison. Thanks for everything, Larry."

* * *

As the late evening train pulled into the station, Mary Jo sat on a bench in a beautiful white southern-style dress. Her healthy face was lit with a smile as she anticipated the adventure before her. Having successfully eluded the searchers, she had circled back home to grab a bite to eat, change, and pack her suitcase.

"Can I get your luggage, ma'am?" The conductor said as she walked toward the train.

"Please," she replied, warming his heart with a coquettish smile. "Thank you very much."

Standing up, she passed through the open door of the Amtrak train and headed for an empty seat.

"All aboard," the conductor called as he followed her up the steps and closed the doors. The train slowly left the station as Mary Jo settled into her seat and thought about all the new playmates she would find as she journeyed across the country.

www.ingramcontent.com/pod-product-compliance
Lightning Source LLC
Chambersburg PA
CBHW022125170626
46808CB00002B/849